The Rainbow Animal

by

Oliver Eade

Silver Quill Publishing
www.silverquillpublishing.com

Silver Quill Publishing

Dedicated to Lucia, Beatriz, Olivia & Lara

In memory of Waffles, a peace-loving hamster.

Acknowledgements

I am forever grateful to my wife, Yvonne Wei-Lun, for her encouragement and endless patience, and also wish to thank all in Silver Quill Publishing for all their encouragement and support.

Carousel or Merry-go-round?

When my Texan granddaughters were younger, my wife and I would sometimes treat them to rides on a wonderful old carousel in a nearby shopping mall in Houston. Often referred to as 'merry-go-rounds' in Britain, in America they were once very popular and, so beautifully built, truly fabulous works of art. Many surviving American and European carousels still use galloping horses for the rides, reflecting their medieval origins as devices for jousting practice and, subsequently, cavalry exercises.

The word carousel derives from the Spanish 'carosella' meaning 'little battle'. Later, carousels appeared in fairgrounds across Europe and the USA for the enjoyment of the public, particularly children. Earlier versions were without platforms and had the horses hanging from chains, allowing the rider to swing out because of centrifugal force. Some were pulled round by hand or by ponies, though later models were driven by steam power and, nowadays, by electricity, with colourful lights and music added. Horses are frequently replaced by various other animals such as those that were ridden by our granddaughters in Texas.

One day, whilst watching our youngest (back then) granddaughter going round and round (*was she on a hippo or was it a lion?*), I began to wonder. I had probably been reading too many science magazines about parallel worlds and quantum universes, but I do remember thinking '*what if that particular animal, hippo or lion, is somehow linked to another dimension. Just suppose the girl and the animal she's sitting on are no longer there after the next time the carousel goes round...'*

Thankfully, she was, but this is how the story of the 'Rainbow Animal' came to be. With a horrific war having been forced upon the citizens of Ukraine, the story has, of course, a more serious side to it as reflected in the words of the late John F. Kennedy.

Chapter 1

"You're far too old for the carousel, Rachel. Why, a girl your age ought to be out socialising."

Socialising?

Of course Rachel knew what it meant, but how she hated the way her mother used big words all the time now as if being a kid was no longer acceptable. Besides, there was something special about the carousel at their local shopping mall in Houston, Texas. Because of the animals. Over the years they had become her friends. Isn't sitting on a friend socialising?

"But Mommy, you promised we'd go to the mall this weekend and it's Sunday already!" the girl moaned, worrying she would not get her weekly ride on one of her animal friends. "There must be something you need to buy. What about Daddy's birthday next week? Getting a present's a real social thing to do, you know."

"Oh my! Thank heaven you reminded me, Rachel. Okay, but just one animal this week."

It was to be a *very* special ride because of something Rachel would have to keep secret from her mommy. She was going to give her pet golden hamster, Waffles, a ride for his birthday present. She'd had him nearly a year and a kid at school had told her that hamsters didn't live much longer than that. He really deserved a present for having been such a good friend to her. If she were to wear her posh, pink dress with a pocket in the front, Waffles could stay hidden. She would be the only one to know he was there.

"Why are you wearing that dress to the mall, Rachel?" her mother asked when she came downstairs. "It's not suitable. Go change into jeans or something."

"But Mommy, you just said I should socialise. So I've got to look posh to socialise. I might meet friends from school at the mall."

"Oh Rachel! What are we going to do with you, honey? All right, then. We leave in ten minutes."

On the way to the mall, wearing a pink hairband in her long black hair, and with Waffles hidden in her dress pocket, Rachel began to think about all those carousel animals. Which, she wondered, would Waffles most enjoy riding on for his big day? There were so many from which to choose: the white tiger, the polar bear, the elephant, the ostrich, the antelope, not to mention the various horses with their beautiful, coloured bridles and saddles. There was even a sea horse. She adored riding the sea horse. But which of these animals would be Waffles' preference? And how on earth could she talk to him about it whilst sitting next to her mommy in the car? Talking to her dress could hardly pass as socialising. No, she would have to make the decision herself for the little hamster.

Waffles tickled her tummy, making her giggle. She

glanced anxiously at her mother.

"What's the joke, dear?"

"Nothing, Mommy. Just something I thought of."

Although Rachel had never seen a '*No Hamsters Allowed*' sign at the carousel, she had a feeling Waffles' presence there would not be properly appreciated. She would have to keep him hidden, which seemed so unfair seeing that the carousel was all about animals!

Concentrating on images of her animal friends in her mind helped Rachel to control the giggles whenever Waffles' nose tickled her tummy. She thought about the lion and imagined herself roaring, for she always liked to pretend she really *was* the animal she had chosen. Rachel-the-lion would leap onto the back of the zebra in front, and woe betide any kid who happened to be sitting astride the zebra. Of course, if she were on the zebra it would be a different matter. The zebra would run as fast as the wind and make a whinnying noise (Rachel thought zebras probably did whinny, although she wasn't sure), and the lion would never catch her. Riding the camel, she would be crossing a hot, dry desert in search of ancient treasure hidden inside the tomb of a long-forgotten pharaoh, or, as a tiger, she might stalk a jungle deer or, as a sleepy hippo, bask in a warm African river.

By the time their car arrived at the mall, Rachel had narrowed the choice down to two animals. Either she would take Waffles for a ride on the polar bear, and they could imagine themselves swimming in the ice-cold Arctic, or it would be an amazing chase across a sun-baked savannah on the back of the cheetah. She just prayed he would not fall asleep and miss the fun. Having fed him well before leaving the house, his cheek pouches were still near to bursting and he usually had a little snooze after a big meal.

As they approached the carousel, Rachel felt so excited for Waffles. He was tickling her tummy again which, thank goodness, meant that he was awake. She looked for the polar bear and the cheetah, then froze...

"Hurry up and decide, Rachel. I must get on with choosing a present for Daddy. What's it to be today? Giraffe? Elephant?"

Rachel did not answer. No longer was she interested in the polar bear or cheetah. Her attention was focused on a weird and colourful creature she had never seen before. How could she have missed it after visiting the carousel so many times? It was such a strange-looking beast, and all the colours of the rainbow. Its head, which resembled that of a kindly lion, was a patchwork of red, yellow and purple and its eyes were a lovely royal blue. The red around its ears blended with a shaggy orange, red and pink mane. A single horn, the same pink as Rachel's dress, stuck out from its forehead like that of a unicorn. Its body, with sturdy red and blue legs, was that of a lion, but the stripy yellow tail reminded Rachel of a tiger.

"The Rainbow Animal!" she whispered to herself.

"Do make up your mind," urged her mommy. "Giraffe or elephant, Rachel?"

"That one!" the girl replied, pointing at the extraordinary creature.

"Sure thing, honey! I'll wait on the bench," Mommy

said, without looking.

She always sat on the same bench. Rachel skipped across to the carousel, causing Waffles to bob about inside her dress pocket. She paid the woman at the kiosk and, as she climbed up onto the back of the Rainbow Animal, she saw her mommy hurry off to the rest room.

"Well, that's why she was so impatient!" she told Waffles.

The girl felt a twinge of embarrassment on spotting Alec, the class nerd, seated on the zebra. She feared he might think that she had been talking to herself.

Alec was the last person on earth with whom she would wish to socialise. Annoyingly, she often saw him at the carousel, but that had never put her off. She would merely look the other way and pretend he wasn't there. Always top of the class in all subjects, the boy was most definitely a geek. Because Alec wore grey, and hardly ever spoke, some of Rachel's classmates claimed his parents were witches. Whatever, she did not want him to go telling other kids at school she was in the habit of having conversations alone. After all, *he* didn't know Waffles was safely tucked away inside her dress pocket.

Whilst she sat on the Rainbow Animal, waiting for the carousel to start up, there was something else Rachel noticed. Most of the carousel animals were hard and you would not want to sit on them for too long or your butt would get sore, but the Rainbow Animal was soft, like a real animal, and felt kind of warm, as if alive.

The carousel music started up and Rachel and Waffles began to move forwards together on the weird multi-coloured creature, up, down and up, slowly at first then rapidly accelerating. Soon they were zipping round. Rachel saw her mommy emerge from the rest room and sit down on the bench. She waved. Funnily, her mommy did not appear to see her. Frowning, the woman stared at the carousel as if wondering where Rachel had got to.

Oh well, just as long as she doesn't know Waffles is sitting in my pocket, the girl thought.

The carousel spun faster and faster until her mommy became just a fuzzy blue smudge. Clutching the pole, Rachel dared not let go to wave again for fear of falling off. Never before had the carousel gone so fast and she prayed that Waffles would not throw up in her pocket. Then something strange happened. The music changed. The carousel organ turned into a brass band playing military music. Something else, too. They were no longer inside the shopping mall. She could not work out exactly where they were, for, like her mommy, everything seemed blurred as they whizzed round and round, but she *was* certain of one thing. Because of the bright blue sky above they were definitely outside and no longer in the mall. It wasn't until the carousel had slowed down again that she realised they were at the top of a steep purple hill. On coming to a standstill, Rachel remained seated, trembling. Not only was there no mall, but the bench with her mommy on it had disappeared.

"Don't be frightened. I know you're a very brave hamster," she reassured Waffles when he nudged her tummy and patted the inside of her pocket with his paws. Saying this out loud gave Rachel courage. Besides, it was

Waffles' birthday present and she could not have him feeling scared. "Just a little adventure," she added, crossing her fingers.

The brass band stopped after the carousel came to a halt. It felt eerily quiet when Rachel climbed down from the Rainbow Animal. She took Waffles out and gently stroked his small head, holding him up so that he could view the awesome scene stretched out before them. Although terrified, she still reckoned this was the most beautiful place she had ever visited.

Chapter 2

The grass that Rachel stood on was bright purple, not green, and there were thousands of yellow, blue and orange flowers dotted about. A little way off was a red path that led down the hill towards a town of amazing buildings, each painted a different colour. A kaleidoscope of blues, yellows, pinks, reds, greens, purples. In fact, every conceivable shade of colour Rachel had ever seen. Like the Rainbow Animal.

Military music started up again. On turning, the girl saw that the Rainbow Animal was moving again. No way could she get back on. She and Waffles were stranded in this weird place. As fear gripped her insides, her knees went all wobbly as if her legs had turned into rubber.

"Hey, look at that, Waffles!" Rachel exclaimed, trying to sound cheerful to hide her fear. She pointed the hamster in the direction of the town. "Have you ever seen anything so fantastical?" Using long words always made her feel braver.

Waffles twitched his nose, and for a few moments the girl worried he might throw up. She rubbed his tummy because she knew he found this comforting whenever he was upset. Concentrating all her attention on Waffles gave her courage helped to make her legs less rubbery.

"There, there," she whispered. "We'll take a rest then get back on the carousel next time it stops. I'll ask them to go more slowly on the way back. Sure they'll understand that was way too fast for a little hamster!"

But what if the carousel failed to stop again? There was no one around she could ask. And what had happened to Alec? When the zebra flashed past, there was no one on it.

Rachel looked up, gaping in wonder at the town down there at the foot of the hill, for the people milling about in the streets were as brightly coloured as the houses. On the other side of the town was a broad, blue-grey river, but beyond this no colour at all. There was another town there, but it could not have been more different from the one at the bottom of the purple hill. The buildings were all either black, grey or white and... well, kind of dull looking. Curiously, the town on Rachel's side of the river had no black, white or grey. She could see two bridges spanning the river, One painted purple, yellow and orange and the other black and white.

The girl saw a dark grey path leading up from the colourless bridge towards the left where it was hidden by the purple hill. She walked slowly around the carousel to get a better view of this path. The purple grass ended abruptly. Here, the hill was covered with grey gravel. She now saw the grey path better as it snaked its way up the gravel slope to the carousel. Half-way down were two grey figures. The smaller was definitely Alec. She recognised him from his untidy black hair, grey shirt and grey trousers. Anyone else and she would have called out to him, but Alec the class nerd and, according to kids at school, the son of witches? No way! The girl turned to run back to her side of the carousel when... BUMP!

Colliding with something plump and red, she almost dropped Waffles. She took a step back. In front of her stood a stout little man dressed in red, his hair the colour of a cardinal's robe, his face that of a tomato. Not a hot and flustered sort of red but most definitely painted, and he was puffing as if he'd just run a marathon.

"Oh dear, oh dear! This hill is far too steep," he panted. "Something should be done about it. They really ought to make it less steep. I ran as fast as I could to get to you in time but I'd have been a lot faster if only they'd fix this hill."

Rachel shielded Waffles' eyes from him in case the hamster should find a totally red person scary. He wore a crimson policeman's uniform and gave her the impression of being someone who had been given authority but did not know what to do with it. He also seemed intensely annoyed with himself for being so breathless. He had obviously run as fast as possible but had still arrived late despite all that puffing and panting. Rachel, a superb runner, would have thought nothing of running up the same hill.

"Dear, dear, dear!" he repeated. "They really *must* do something about this hill. I'll have to bring it to the president's attention."

The girl could not think how you could make a hill less steep, or why the president, whoever he was, would want to involve himself in such matters. In fact, she thought it would have been better if they, whoever they were, had sent someone who could run faster uphill.

"So glad... *puff, puff*... you made it," the little man said between deep breaths whilst peering anxiously at Rachel's hair. "You're only... *puff, puff*... just in time... but... *puff, puff*... oh dear, dear, dear!" He began to blink frantically.

"Are you all right?" Rachel asked. "And 'just in time' for what?"

"It's black!" the man exclaimed, ignoring her second question. "It can't be. That'll never do. We'll have to fix it. But of course. How silly of me. Your dress. It's pink. Your hairband, too. We'll get Mrs Pink to change it for you. Your hair, that is."

"Why would you want to do that? And you still haven't said what we're 'just in time' for," protested Rachel feeling more than a little bit cross. The thought of having pink hair did not appeal.

"Why, the war with the Dullabillies, of course. Battle commences at eight twenty-four tomorrow morning. Brought forward a day. And we've so much to discuss before then."

"We?" questioned Rachel, puzzled.

"Yes, indeed," the man said. "You, our new military advisor, together with President Banana, Sergeant Lobster and myself. I'm Sheriff Tomato, by the way. And so very glad you're here... erm... whatever your name is."

The little fellow held out a red hand to shake Rachel's, which was kind of awkward because the girl's hand that wasn't holding Waffles covered her broadening grin after hearing he was called Sheriff Tomato. She desperately tried to stop giggling as they shook hands.

"My name's Rachel, actually. And this is Waffles," she added, holding Waffles up in front of the man's red face.

Sheriff Tomato bowed respectfully.

"Military Advisor Rachel, I'm mighty pleased to make your acquaintance. And that of your... erm... your assistant, Waffles."

"Sheriff Tomato, there must be some kind of mistake. I..."

"No time for mistakes," he interrupted. "Come quickly! Can't keep the President waiting. Oh dear, your hair. I just don't understand it. Better see what Mrs Pink can do first. Your lodgings are with her, anyway."

"Lodgings?" queried Rachel, returning Waffles to her pocket. She hurried after Sheriff Tomato when, ignoring her query, he promptly took off along the red path. She soon discovered that he could go pretty fast downhill.

"Yes, yes," he replied. "Rachel, huh? Funny name, but I suppose it has to be pink. Because of your dress. And your hairband."

"What do you mean my name has to be pink? It's not any colour. It's just Rachel."

"Yes, indeed! Rachel. Pink," insisted Sheriff Tomato. "It's so inconvenient about your hair, you know. They should've fixed it before sending you. *And* your shoes. We'll have to make them pink as well."

"But you can't dye my hair and shoes pink," the girl protested. "Mommy would be furious. Besides, I've got lots of other clothes and shoes back home and they're all sorts of colours."

"All sorts of colours?" queried Sheriff Tomato, panting

as they ran together down the red path. "Indeed! Not far now," he added on approaching the first row of colourful houses. "And welcome to Colorwallytown."

"Colorwallytown?" questioned Rachel.

"Yes. As I said, the battle with Dullabillieville starts tomorrow at eight twenty-four sharp. We're relying on you, Advisor Rachel. You'll help us lick 'em into shape, huh? Easy victory for a military advisor of your experience, no doubt!"

"Look, I'm only a—" began Rachel, but Sheriff Tomato interrupted her before she could say 'schoolgirl from Houston'. "There, at the bottom of that street on the right," he informed her.

Rachel chased after Sheriff Tomato whilst he trotted along the bright orange sidewalk towards a pink cottage at the far end of a side street.

She had never before seen such colour. The roads and sidewalks were like patchwork quilts, as were the houses, and the gardens in front of those beautiful houses looked unreal. Some had purple lawns, like the carousel hill, some red, some yellow, and, to her surprise, there were a few with green lawns. The flowers in the gardens were awesome. Better than any flower shop her mommy had taken her to. As she ran alongside Sheriff Tomato—and she didn't dare run too fast for fear Waffles might bounce out of her dress pocket—they passed women and children whose faces and hands were all painted brilliant blue, mauve, orange, yellow, every bit as colourful as the flowers in the gardens. They had dyed hair and their clothes and shoes were also brightly coloured. Many stopped and looked at Rachel in a puzzled sort of a way.

"Why are they all staring at me like that?" she asked Sheriff Tomato.

"It's... *puff, puff...* your hair... and... *puff, puff...* um... your shoes, Advisor Rachel," he explained.

Rachel reckoned she should perhaps have her black hair and her white shoes made pink if only to stop the Colorwallies from gawping. But this would *really* give Alec something to tease her about at school the following day should he catch sight of her. How she prayed they would never meet up in this strange place.

Chapter 3

Sheriff Tomato was still puffing like an old steam engine as he knocked impatiently on the door of the pink cottage. Rachel removed Waffles from her pocket to check that he was all right. Stroking the hamster, she reassured him everything was going to be just fine. She told him she might soon look a little different with pink hair, but not to worry. Waffles responded by looking up at her and twitching his nose. When the door opened to reveal a short, little lady with a bright pink, jolly face, she returned him to the hamster to her pocket.

Like Sheriff Tomato, Mrs Pink was well-rounded and wore a pink apron and a dress of a slightly darker shade than Rachel's. Her hair was pink too. Rachel's heart sank. To think she might soon look like that. But the woman smiled, and Rachel cheered up for that smile was the friendliest she had ever seen.

"I've been so looking forward to meeting you," Mrs Pink announced, giving the girl a warm hug. Rachel worried that she might have squashed Waffles, but when she checked on him, he didn't appear too flattened. Only a little bit surprised.

"Advisor Rachel needs... erm..." Sheriff Tomato began to blink again and Rachel felt certain he had turned a shade redder. "She needs... erm... her hair. Yes. Her hair and her shoes. Thank you, Mrs Pink. Thank you *very* much!"

He gave a dignified bow. Mrs Pink winked at Rachel and shrugged her shoulders. As she showed the girl into the cosy cottage, she whispered, "I think your hair's lovely, my dear, but I know what he means."

"I'll wait outside, Mrs Pink," suggested Sheriff Tomato. "Thank you!"

The sheriff never seemed to smile, and this only made Rachel want to giggle all the more.

"Don't worry, Rachel," Mrs Pink said, on closing the front door behind the sheriff. "We Colorwallies all have to dye our hair unless it happens to be yellow or red. It's the law and it wouldn't do for President Banana to see your beautiful, black hair. We can wash it off at a later date. Your face and hands, though, they're pink enough as they are."

Everything in Mrs Pink's neat and tidy little cottage was a brightly cheerful colour, mostly pink, and Rachel loved the pretty-patterned wallpaper. The woman led her into a tidy, little kitchen.

"You must be starving," she said.

"Well, I am kind of hungry. Mommy usually buys me a cookie after a ride on the carousel."

"You've a mommy? Oh, how wonderful! Sit there at the table, my dear. I'll fetch some cake and then get everything ready for your hair."

"I do love cake," announced Rachel, her mouth-watering at the mention of food. "Can Waffles have some too, please?"

She took the hamster out of her pocket and tickled his head.

"Waffles?" questioned Mrs Pink, peering at the little hamster.

The girl held out her hand. Mrs Pink stared in surprise. Waffles sat on her palm twitching his nose and staring up at the pink woman.

"Well, I never!" exclaimed Mrs Pink. "What a funny little creature."

Rachel laughed.

"He's a golden hamster," she explained. "His name's Waffles."

"Can he talk?"

Rachel laughed again.

"Nope, I'm afraid not, but I'm sure he understands me. So I talk to him. Sometimes Mommy and Daddy think I'm silly when I tell him things, though."

"I'm sure you're never silly, Rachel. Not if you're our Military Advisor."

"But Mrs Pink, I think—"

"Why are his cheeks so fat?" interrupted the woman, squinting at Waffles' pouches.

"He stores food in them," replied Rachel. "All hamsters do that. But it's okay. He can still eat some cake now and enjoy it later."

"How clever of him! And I don't think he needs to be dyed. He's such a lovely golden colour already."

Mrs Pink took a magnificent pink, orange and lavender cake down from a shelf and cut two slices. A large one for

17

Rachel and a small piece for Waffles. She put them on a pink plate in front of Rachel. The girl placed Waffles on the table and gave him his piece. It quickly disappeared into one of his pouches. She took one bite out of her piece of cake and her eyes popped wide open for it was simply scrumptious.

"Best cake I've ever had, Mrs Pink!" she declared when she had finished relishing that first mouthful. Mrs Pink was already busily stirring pale pink powder into a bowl of warm water.

"Oh, thank you kindly, my dear," the woman said, grinning.

"Mrs Pink, what's all this about a war tomorrow?"

"That's why you're here. Now don't you go telling the sheriff that I said this, but I think it's all completely crazy. Those men, though, they will not listen to us women, you know. I'm just so glad they've got a girl to be our military advisor."

"Mrs Pink, I don't know anything about wars and stuff. Neither does Waffles."

"Well, my dear, perhaps that's a good thing. You'll make them all see sense, huh?"

"Who *are* the Dullabillies, anyway?"

"Once they were our friends. And just the same as us, they would be, if we washed off all our colour and they got rid of the black and white stuff their laws say they have to put on. They're not allowed any colour at all in that town of theirs but our laws say we absolutely *must* have colour. Everywhere!"

"Sounds weird if you ask me," said Rachel, before

stuffing more cake into her mouth.

"That's what this war's all about, I'm afraid. They don't like looking across the river and seeing our colourful streets and buildings and our lot are fed up with staring at their dull black and white town. And then there are the fish."

"The fish?"

Rachel looked baffled. Surely they weren't going to war over fish?

"The fishermen on our side, they fish for black and white and grey fish in the river. After catching them they put them in bowls, take them downstream and let them go."

"Why? Don't you eat fish in Colorwallytown? I really love fish fingers."

"Oh no! Not the black and white ones. Couldn't do that. It's against the law. But that's the trouble. The coloured fish that we *can* eat, the pink and red and gold ones, their fisherman catch these and take them downstream too. Our fishermen complain that they have to go too far to get enough coloured fish to sell because the Dullabillie fishermen keep removing them, and the Dullabillies say the same about our fishermen with the black and white fish."

"I think that's really silly!"

"So do I, my dear! And now that you've finished your cake we can put this bowl on the table... just so!" Mrs Pink took away the plate and placed the bowl in front of Rachel. "Lean forwards and let your hair drop into the dye. There. Perfect. Stay like this for a few minutes. And rub it in well."

Rachel pulled a face as Mrs Pink worked the pink dye into her hair with strong, stubby fingers. "Three minutes should do. Whilst I go and get your room ready. Be back really quick, I will."

Rachel sat with her head forwards and her eyes closed, her long hair floating in the warm, pink dye. She was trying to make sense of what was happening when she felt something tap her nose. Opening her eyes, she looked down. It was Waffles. She'd forgotten all about him. After wandering about on the table, he had obviously decided to jump into the pink dye, have a swim then panicked. His tiny pink face peered anxiously up at her. He reached out with a paw to draw attention to himself, as if trying to say 'hey, help me!'

"Waffles... you're all pink!" Rachel exclaimed before removing the dripping hamster from the bowl. "My, you do look odd. For a hamster, anyway... oh my gosh!"

She'd just seen her hair which was the same vivid pink as Waffles. When Mrs Pink reappeared with a pink towel, Rachel was shaking the pink dye from her pink hair over the bowl, and a pink Waffles was padding about making little pink paw prints on the pink table.

"Oh... you needn't have made *him* pink as well, my dear," said Mrs Pink.

"Didn't mean to," explained Rachel, wiping dye from her eyes. "He just jumped in for a swim and turned pink."

"Not to worry. Now dry your hair and take off those shoes. I'll make them pink too. To match your hair and your assistant."

Mrs Pink, bursting with energy, bustled off with

Rachel's shoes, leaving the girl to dry herself and Waffles. She returned shortly with a pair of dark pink shoes. Rachel wasn't sure about the colour. In fact, she wasn't sure about anything, *particularly* her pink hair and pink hamster. However, she did not wish to hurt Mrs Pink's feelings. After all, the woman was only doing what she had been told to do. To make sure that there was nothing whatsoever black, white or grey about Rachel, the new Colorwally military advisor.

But what if she were to bump into Alec?

Chapter 4

Actually, Rachel did not think Alec was as bad as some kids made out. He could not help being a nerd if he was brainy. Just a bit of a loner, she reckoned, and she wasn't sure she believed in all that witch business. But the real problem was that he might tell others at school about her pink hair.

"Those Dullabillies, they're not kind of witches or something, are they?" she asked Mrs Pink, with a slight frown. "Only I saw a boy I know from—"

"Witches? Why do you ask?" interrupted Mrs Pink. She seemed worried.

"Well, I don't really believe in witches. And I'm sure Alec's parents aren't witches, either."

"You don't believe in witches? But that's why we're Colorwallies. To keep the witches out. We know that they're always black or grey or white. So, we'd recognise them straightaway in Colorwallytown, wouldn't we? They'd stand out. That's what our president says, anyhow."

"But what if there aren't such things as witches?" asked Rachel, frowning again. "Then you're all wasting your time and there'd be no need for a war." She paused in thought. "But if the Dullabillies *aren't* witches, then why... erm...?"

she asked, feeling puzzled.

"Why do *they* ban colour across the river? Simple, my dear. Over there they believe that witches paint themselves funny colours for disguise. Red, green, blue... whatever. They keep saying we could be harbouring witches here without knowing it. And our leaders say the same about them. Oh dear, all I want is for this war to be over!"

Waffles was already back in Rachel's dress pocket when the girl heard a knock at the door. Sheriff Tomato had returned.

"Perfect!" he announced on seeing Rachel. And he smiled, which made Rachel want to giggle for his face went all wrinkly and she had never before seen a large, wrinkled tomato.

"Now you be sure to look after her properly," Mrs Pink warned the sheriff.

"Yes, yes! Of course, Mrs Pink. I'll bring her straight back to you after we've had our Council of War with the president, Sergeant Lobster and, um, the general."

As they set off, running through the colourful streets of Colorwallytown, Rachel was thinking the Council of War sounded a little scary. Anyway, she did attract fewer stares with her hair and shoes being pink. Waffles occasionally poked his little face over the edge of her pocket, but he was now so well camouflaged against his owner's pink dress no one seemed to notice him.

After a short jog, and on turning a corner, Rachel saw the most incredible building.

"The Presidential Palace!" Sheriff Tomato proudly announced.

Rachel's jaw dropped. She had never seen such a beautiful palace. To tell the truth, she had not actually seen *any* real palaces because they didn't have such things in Houston, Texas—only pictures in books and in movies—but she had no idea they could be so awesome.

With its five floors, the only tallish building in Colorwallytown, the palace façade was painted with elaborate designs in so many tints and hues that the girl's eyes almost popped out as she tried to count them. The roof alone was a mix of purple, yellow and blue, with a central gold tower. In front of the main door stood two yellow-faced guards in green, pink and gold uniforms. The gardens surrounding the palace had lawns of the same purple grass as the carousel hill, and the flower beds were simply bursting with flowers of all shapes and colours. Rachel could not help but think how awful it would be if their enemy in this stupid war, the Dullabillies, were to destroy the wonderful building. And all because of fish and witches which she felt sure did not even exist.

But what if she was wrong, and the kids at school were right, about Alec? And what if witches were to infiltrate Colorwallytown, cast spells on people and turn Mrs Pink grey, white or black?

Sheriff Tomato approached the golden gates of the palace. One of the yellow-faced guards came forward and opened them, bowing to Rachel and Waffles who, now curious, peered out from her pocket, then up at the sheriff.

"Sheriff Tomato, can we stop this war?" Rachel asked as they accompanied the guards to the palace doors. "I mean, I'm not sure I believe in witches. At least, I don't think I do."

"Out of the question!" the man snapped. "Absolutely out of the question!" She noticed his eyelids blink again. They seemed to do that whenever he was either upset or confused about something. "You see, it all began when the Dullabillie Ambassador, Greywolf, demanded that we paint our houses along the riverside a dull grey, white or black and make sure people using the riverside walk have no colour about them," he explained. "President Banana said only on condition that the Dullabillies paint *their* riverfront houses bright and cheerful colours and allow only colourful people on *their* riverside walk. Greywolf did not like this one little bit. He went across the Dullabillie bridge to see President Coalface and returned a day early with an ultimatum. Yesterday. We didn't expect him back till tomorrow."

He paused thoughtfully. The blinking stopped.

"The ultimatum was that if we Colorwallies fail to agree to paint at least every other riverfront house grey, white or black, unconditionally, then war will break out between our two towns. Our president couldn't possibly agree to this, so ambassadors were exchanged this morning. At eight twenty-four tomorrow, the battle begins. Thank heavens you got here a day early! We were afraid you wouldn't arrive till after the fighting had started, and General Greengage... well, you'll meet him soon... he's well... Yes, yes... he's General Greengage, you see. You'll know what I mean at the Council of War. Hmm!"

"I heard all about the fish and the witches," said Rachel, "and I think it's crazy. Even if there *are* such things

25

as witches."

"Ah, but what about the grey and white fishes? They could be cursed by witches, Advisor Rachel," cautioned Sheriff Tomato, blinking again as they approached the palace door. The two guards whispered to each other. One turned, bowed and addressed Rachel:

"I do hope Advisor Rachel won't feel too inconvenienced if she is requested to wait a bit. The, um... the First Lady Violet is still... um... looking for her violet nail polish to apply before she feels able to receive such a distinguished guest as yourself."

The sheriff went very red indeed and blinked like the wings of a hummingbird. Rachel felt truly sorry for him.

"Oh, that's all right," she said to the guard. "I'm quite happy to wait here. I do enjoy talking to Sheriff Tomato."

This helped the sheriff to relax and he stopped blinking. As the guard who had spoken was about to disappear through the grand palatial entrance, Rachel called after him...

"Sometimes my mommy keeps her nail polish in her purse. The First Lady should look in *her* purse."

"Oh, thank you, Advisor Rachel. I'll convey your advice to the First Lady."

Rachel spoke again to the sheriff:

"My Aunty Jessica has a lovely white house, you know, and she most definitely is not a witch." The sheriff went quiet. *Oh dear*, thought the girl, *I've gone and said the wrong thing*. "But she has got a stars and stripes in the front yard," she added to cheer him up.

"Stars and stripes?" queried Sheriff Tomato. He

sounded alarmed.

"Sure!" Rachel nodded. "The American Flag. It's got lots of blue and red in it."

"There you go, then," said the sheriff. He looked happier. "Blue and red! Not a witch."

"And she has gorgeous colourful flowers in her yard."

"Even better."

"But I do rather... um... like her white house."

The Sheriff began to blink.

Oh, please hurry up, Mr Guard, thought Rachel. *I'm not doing very well with this conversation.*

She wished Waffles could take over and say something helpful, but all he seemed able to do was to squeak.

"Why is this war going to start at eight twenty-four and not eight twenty-five or eight thirty?" Rachel asked, eager to change the subject.

"Probably it's the time at which the Dullabillie First Lady, Snow White, has to set her alarm so that she can feed her cat, Sooty, in time," came the unhelpful reply.

"In time for what?" questioned Rachel. She was beginning to think that in many ways the Colorwallies and the Dullabillies must be rather similar.

"In time to have her nails painted white, just before," replied the agitated sheriff.

"Before *what*?" queried Rachel, beginning to feel a little annoyed.

"Before making breakfast, after," the little man answered before pausing yet again.

"What?"

"*What?*"

"After what?"

"After the Dullabillie president, President Coalface, gets up at eight twenty-nine. When…"

"When?"

"Yes!"

"When what?"

"When Sheriff Nightsky reports to him that…"

Sheriff Tomato went quiet. Rachel sighed.

"That the Dullabillies have been at war with us Colorwallies since," continued Sheriff Tomato.

"Since eight twenty-four?" suggested the girl.

"Precisely, Advisor Rachel! Excellent! What an intelligent military advisor we have."

Rachel was much relieved when the door re-opened and the yellow-faced guard reappeared.

"Advisor Rachel was quite correct," the man announced. "The First Lady's nail polish was in her purse. Please enter. The President is ready to hold the Council of War."

By now, Rachel no longer felt nervous about going to a Council of War as a military advisor. In fact, she had a good mind to tell them that the whole thing was a load of poppycock and a serious waste of everyone's time, but as they were led through sumptuous hallways and along grand corridors she decided to leave *that* bit of telling to Waffles. Actually, Waffles had gone rather quiet. On peeking into her pocket, she saw that he had fallen fast asleep.

"Too much cake," she muttered, shaking her head.

"What?" Sheriff Tomato asked abruptly as they

climbed a splendid staircase where every stair had been painted a different colour. It was like walking up a rainbow. "You think we should give the Dullabillies too much cake to eat? Send our spies across with free cake for everyone? Give them all a tummy-ache before battle? Brilliant idea, Advisor Rachel! Awesome, in fact! We must tell the President at once."

"No," replied Rachel, struggling not to giggle. "Waffles has eaten too much of Mrs Pink's cake and fallen asleep."

"Oh dear," the Sheriff exclaimed. "We'll have to wake him up. Can't have your assistant snoring in front of President Banana."

At which point Rachel did giggle. Into her hand. But half-way up the stairway she briefly halted, for at the top, flanked by two guards, stood the diminutive President Banana, as yellow as a banana and looking extremely serious. At his side was a totally violet, little woman whom Rachel took to be First Lady Violet. When the girl reached the top of the stairs, the presidential couple bowed as if large bags, heavy with shopping, had just been slung around their necks. Rachel was not used to people bowing to her, and certainly not used to bowing back. The best she could manage was a slight nod whilst Sheriff Tomato almost touched the ground with his mop of red hair.

Chapter 5

"Oh my! I can tell from the girl's face that you've gotten me a wise military advisor, Sheriff Tomato. Wise and extremely clever," proclaimed the President. "I have good feelings about the battle tomorrow, you know. *Very* good feelings."

Rachel did not have good feelings about anything, particularly the battle. In fact, the very mention of war made her feel quite queasy, and she was certain that Waffles was not going to enjoy it. He was most definitely not a fighting kind of hamster.

"Sergeant Lobster, and... um... the general, of course, they're here already. In the Great Hall. So I do believe we're all ready for the Council of War, huh? Advisor Rachel, I would be most honoured if you were to sit beside me at the head of the long table."

The President led Rachel and Waffles along a wide corridor to a vast and beautifully decorated hall lined by mirrors that reflected its thousands of colours, making the place seem even larger.

"If you were to sit beside me, I might feel more important," the President whispered to the girl, out of earshot of the others. "I do like to feel important, you know," he added sheepishly. Rachel wondered whether the two towns were only going to war just to make their presidents feel important, and whether all that silly business about fish and witches was a feeble excuse.

At the far end of the Great Hall was a long gold and blue painted table, and at one end of this sat two colourful figures. One a pinkish red, with a little yellow hat and three yellow chevrons on the sleeve of his red tunic, and the other, a wizened, old, wrinkled, bent green figure of a man. The latter had a pile of coloured brushes in front of him on the table and he appeared to be playing some sort of a private game with them.

"General Greengage and Sergeant Lobster!" announced Sheriff Tomato importantly as they approached the two men. Sergeant Lobster stood and bowed respectfully to Rachel, but the general remained seated, pushing his brushes around in front of him.

"It is indeed an honour," said the sergeant. "We've heard so much about your brilliance in the art of war, Advisor Rachel. Right, General Greengage?"

The general grunted, picked up an orange paintbrush, looked at it then put it back on the table.

"Here, next to me!" the President suggested to Rachel, patting the chair beside him. Sheriff Tomato sat on the other side of Rachel, and First Lady Violet, who kept examining her painted nails, sat on the other side of her husband. By now, Rachel was feeling curious to know what people talked about at Councils of War.

She felt something tickle her tummy and realised

Waffles had woken up.

"Can Waffles listen, too?" she asked.

President Banana leaned behind Rachel and whispered something to Sheriff Tomato. The sheriff started to blink.

"Erm... um... the President wishes to know the colour of Waffles," he announced.

"Oh, pink like me," Rachel replied confidently, hoping his dye hadn't rubbed off onto her dress whilst he'd been asleep.

President Banana smiled and nodded wisely. The girl removed Waffles from her pocket and put him on the table in front of the yellow man. Thankfully, he was still totally pink apart from brown eyes.

"Waffles, be on your very best behaviour, now!" Rachel cautioned.

"Shall we begin, Mr President, ladies and gentlemen?" asked Sheriff Tomato.

Rachel agreed, together with the rest of the company.

"Well, first I think we should allow Advisor Rachel to give us her strategy for the battle tomorrow."

Stunned, Rachel stared blankly ahead. She had no idea what to say. The thought of sending soldiers across that river, armed with guns and rockets and bombs, was abhorrent. She was just about to say as much, and hopefully make a quick escape from the palace and run back up the purple hill to the carousel, when Sergeant Lobster interrupted:

"Perhaps I should first inform Advisor Rachel about the arsenal."

Arsenal?

Rachel had heard the word before, but she wasn't sure what it meant. A place where they kept guns and stuff, she wondered? Sheriff Tomato blinked. He was clearly embarrassed about having failed to inform her about the arsenal.

"Oh dear, oh dear," he muttered, looking anxiously down at the table. "The arsenal... yes, yes. Of course, Sergeant Lobster. Please inform Advisor Rachel. I know I should have, but there again, there was all that... um... that business, well, with the... um... hair... and... um, the shoes. Yes, the shoes. Indeed!"

"And what about..." began Sergeant Lobster, peering over his shoulder as if to check no one else was listening. "...What about the secret weapon?" he added in a quiet voice.

"Most of all the secret weapon, sergeant! Please advise our military advisor. About everything. Thank you!"

"Right! Well, we'll take you to inspect the secret weapon straight after the Council of War, Advisor Rachel, but first I wish to inform you that we have eight hundred and sixty-seven troops. That's not including the general. With the general that makes, um... let me see... eight... um..."

"Eight hundred and sixty-eight?" offered Rachel.

"Brilliant!" exclaimed President Banana. "Absolutely brilliant. I have an extremely good feeling about tomorrow's battle with you in charge of operations."

"Operations? Aren't they what doctors do in hospitals?" asked Rachel. The others all looked at each other, but no one replied.

"They're all different colours. The troops, that is," burbled Sergeant Lobster. "And there are two thousand three hundred and sixty-four... um—"

"What colours are the houses where *you* come from, Advisor Rachel?" interrupted President Banana, plainly bored with Sergeant Lobster's prattling. Rachel was just about to say that her Aunty Jessica had a beautiful white house in Houston, Texas, when the Sheriff butted in...

"Stars and stripes, stars and stripes," he said. "Blue and red. The Houston flag."

"*American* flag," corrected Rachel.

"Indeed, indeed," agreed the little man. "And Mr President, they have lots of flowers in their yards. Very many flowers! All colours."

"Paint brushes!" It was Sergeant Lobster again. They all seemed to have forgotten about him. "Two thousand three hundred and sixty-four paint brushes, eighty-six paint sprayers and..." He looked up at the ceiling, as if struggling with the mental arithmetic. "Um... two hundred and seventy-two pots of paint. All colours. House paint and people paint. That's not counting..." He paused.

"What?" asked Rachel.

"What?" echoed Sergeant Lobster looking confused and a little worried that Rachel might suddenly turn angry.

"Not counting *what*?" the girl asked with irritation.

"The secret weapon," he added in a hushed voice.

Sheriff Tomato started to blink furiously and turned almost beetroot red.

"She doesn't know *any*thing about the secret weapon?"

questioned the sergeant.

The sheriff shook his head, his discomfiture painfully apparent.

"Oh!" exclaimed Rachel. "I thought I should *see* the secret weapon first before I hear about it, didn't I, Sheriff?" She winked at the little man, but he was blinking so fast she could not tell whether or not he winked back at her.

"See it first. Yes, yes," he agreed, and gradually the blinking settled down.

"Do we Colorwallies have an ambassador in Houston?" the President suddenly asked Rachel, as though unaware of the conversation that had been going on.

Rachel's eyes took in the curious little multi-coloured people seated at the long table as she thought about those other Colorwallies she had seen in the streets of Colorwallytown. They all resembled clowns and she remembered having once seen a circus clown called Bobo with a big red nose and lips, red blobs on his cheeks, an orange jacket, baggy trousers and a funny purple hat plus huge, flappy green shoes.

"I think he's called Bobo," she replied.

"Ambassador Bobo!" President Banana repeated. "Excellent!"

"So, Advisor Rachel, your strategy for Mr President, please."

It was Sheriff Tomato. Rachel had no idea what 'strategy' really meant. At least, not in a military sense.

"Could I have some water for Waffles, please?" she asked to give herself time to think. "He's feeling rather thirsty after Mrs Pink's cake."

35

This was true. Whenever Waffles stuck his nose up in the air, as he was now doing, it meant he was thirsty.

"An excellent strategy," agreed President Banana. "Truly excellent! Sheriff Tomato, you are indeed to be congratulated. We have a seriously talented military advisor. After the battle, I shall be considering you for full military honours."

Rachel thought how lucky Sheriff Tomato was because he could blush without it showing. The President called out to one of the yellow-faced guards who, moments later, hurried off to fetch a bowl of water for Waffles. Rachel put the hamster gently down in front of the bowl. There was total silence as they all sat and watched the hamster place his paws on the edge of bowl, stick his nose in the water and begin to lap, making a funny plopping noise. When he twitched at Rachel afterwards, his nose was wet.

"A good start," said the President. "And then?"

Sheriff Tomato gazed with pride at the girl.

"And then I'll see the arsenal," she replied. "That's my strategy."

"Wonderful!" exclaimed President Banana. "So we can call the Council of War to a close. Isn't that terrific, my dear?" he asked First Lady Violet, but she was far too busy examining her fingernails to pay heed.

Sergeant Lobster and Sheriff Tomato stood up together. Rachel popped Waffles back into her dress pocket before rising from her chair. She glanced at General Greengage who was still playing with his brushes.

"I don't think we should disturb the general just now," observed the sheriff. "Needs to conserve his energy for the big day, huh?"

Chapter 6

And so Rachel left the Great Hall with the sheriff and the sergeant. The President remained seated, smiling contentedly, whilst General Greengage just pushed his brushes around on the table with an expression of intense concentration on his wrinkled, green face. Rachel wasn't quite sure what the general thought he was doing. Perhaps he was working out military strategies with the brushes. Or maybe just having fun.

"Who knows?" she whispered to Waffles. Her beloved little hamster was looking sleepy again, so as they left the palace, she made a request. "I think I should put Waffles to bed before I see the arsenal. Could we stop off at Mrs Pink's, please?"

"Of course, Advisor Rachel," exclaimed the sheriff. "An important strategy, that. *Very* important!"

As they headed along colourful street towards Mrs Pink's pretty cottage, Rachel thought that being a military advisor was not so very difficult after all. Almost anything could become a part of her 'strategy'. The sheriff and the sergeant waited outside whilst Rachel went back into the cottage to put Waffles to bed. Of course, he would have to share her own lovely, soft bed with pink sheets and a patterned multi-coloured quilted duvet. When she took him out of her pocket, she saw something that didn't normally belong there. A collection of little pink poops. He must have swallowed some of the dye to turn them pink.

"Thank goodness you didn't do that on the presidential table," she admonished whilst tucking him into bed. She emptied the poops into the pink toilet in the pink en-suite bathroom and returned to the pink kitchen.

"Would you keep an eye on Waffles, please?" she asked Mrs Pink.

"Why of course, my dear!"

"Mrs Pink, where's Mr Pink?" Rachel asked.

"It's a sad story," the woman said, her jolly face turning sorrowful. "I'm afraid he's no longer with us. You see, he died five years ago."

"Oh, I'm so sorry," exclaimed Rachel. She really did feel sorry for Mrs Pink because she was such a nice lady. Tears glistened in the woman's eyes and the girl gave her a hug.

"I've no children, either," added Mrs Pink.

"Well, whilst I'm staying in Colorwallytown, could I kind of be like your kid?" suggested Rachel.

"That's awful sweet of you, my dear, but you'll have your own mommy and daddy."

"Yeah, I guess so." agreed Rachel. "And I miss them really bad." She, too, began to feel sad.

"Of course you do!"

"Mrs Pink, is there something wrong with General Greengage? He does seem a bit strange. Like he's always playing around with brushes."

"It's not something we're supposed to talk about, Rachel, but he's certainly not the man he used to be. Once he was one of our most brilliant generals ever, they say, but... well... that's why you're here, you see. They needed a military advisor because it's all he does now. Play with his brushes. And no one knows why. But I must say I am really glad they've appointed you to replace him, Rachel."

"Why?" the girl asked, for Mrs Pink now had an odd faraway look in her eyes. "I know nothing at all about war. Except that it's horrible."

"Well, there's this man, see," turning to look at Rachel. "He has such a kind face. But he's a Dullabillie. He comes to the market here with his children. Some of the Dullabillies do that. It's against their laws, but they do it all the same. To smuggle colourful toys back across the river 'cos their kids get so sick of black and white and grey ones. I always hope to see him whenever I go to the market." The woman paused. "I even know his name. It's Whitestone. His children are called Snowdrop and Nerino. And he's widowed. If it wasn't for this stupid war, I could... um... You see, I know how difficult it must be for him looking after two children on his own. I thought he might do with a bit of help. That's all. I could cook for him, do their washing and things. When I heard you were to be our new military advisor, I thought perhaps you might end this war quickly so that..." Mrs Pink went quiet and looked embarrassed.

"Do you want to marry him?"

Mrs Pink didn't answer. Instead, she just looked sad.

"Hurry!" she urged. "Can't keep the sheriff and the sergeant waiting while we chat. I'll see you later, my dear, and tomorrow you must have a real good breakfast. In preparation for the big day, huh?"

Happy that Waffles would be in good hands whilst she was gone, Rachel left Mrs Pink's cottage and followed Sheriff Tomato and Sergeant Lobster along the colourful Colorwallytown streets to a large yellow and blue building with 'ARSENAL' written in bold red letters above a massive orange metal door.

The sergeant banged on the door, three times, with his fist. Each echoing 'boom' shook Rachel's bones. The door creaked open, slowly...

Chapter 7

Rachel was just about to scold Sergeant Lobster for frightening her when he suggested she might wish to survey the troops before seeing the secret weapon.

"I'll get them all lined up for you with their paint brushes at the ready," he added.

Paint brushes?

For some reason, the girl found this extremely funny. She tried to do mental arithmetic in her head as she fought to suppress her giggles. She was very good at math and had discovered that doing difficult long division sums in her head was a good way to focus her mind and prevent her from collapsing into giggles. So, she tried to work out a particularly hard sum in her head whilst avoiding eye-contact with the funny little red-faced men.

"General Greengage should survey the troops himself, of course, but I'm afraid he's far too busy re-arranging his brushes," continued Sergeant Lobster.

"Eleven point two seven!" blurted Rachel, the answer to her sum, as she tried so very hard not to laugh.

"Wonderful!" Sheriff Tomato exclaimed. "The code for the Secret Weapon! I'll write that down."

Rachel had no idea what he was talking about. She thought up another difficult long-division sum as the sheriff took out an orange notepad and green pencil and wrote down '11.27' which was the answer to the one she had just worked out in her head. The door opened and the sergeant disappeared inside the building, only to reappear moments later.

"The troops are ready, Advisor Rachel," he announced.

When Rachel entered the arsenal and saw row upon row of colourful soldiers standing to attention, with giant paintbrushes resting on their shoulders as soldiers back home would have borne rifles, it was too much. She collapsed with the giggles. Sheriff Tomato began to blink like crazy and that only made her giggle even more. At the same time, she felt bad about upsetting him for he now looked seriously troubled.

"Something's tickling me," she lied. "I think a caterpillar must have just crawled under my dress or something."

"Oh dear, I hope it's not one of those black and white ones," the Sheriff said. "We Tomatoes are so quite allergic to them, you know."

Which proved to be the last straw for the girl. An allergic tomato?

Rachel had to rush outside where she leant against the blue and yellow wall and took in deep breaths to control her laughter. When she had finally settled down, she went back in to get on with the job of surveying the troops. She walked up and down in front of the lines of soldiers who stood with their brushes at the ready. Some also held large paint sprayers. Sergeant Lobster proudly showed her tins of paint of every possible colour along the shelves lining the walls of the arsenal. What an incredible scene it was.

And what a shame that it's all to do with a stupid war, thought Rachel.

"Shall we?" asked Sheriff Tomato of Rachel.

"Shall we what?" responded Rachel.

"Show you?"

"What?"

"How!"

"How what?"

"It works."

"What?"

"With…"

"With what?"

"With the secret code you gave me. I wrote it down."

"But that was just the answer to—"

"It's in a locked room at the other end of the hall," interrupted the sheriff. "Do you have the key, Sergeant?"

"I thought *you* had it, Sheriff," the sergeant replied. "Don't you remember? I said, 'There it is' when we were here with General Greengage."

"But… oh dear, oh dear! I saw the general put something into a pot of turquoise paint. Do you think, erm…?" The sheriff's blinking started up again. "I'll lose my job, I'm sure I shall, if the key is lost. I'm done for. We must find that key!"

"Don't worry, I'll sort this out," reassured Rachel. The girl went over to the nearest line of soldiers. "Now, I want you lot to find the key to the door for the room with the secret weapon. That's part of our strategy. You ten guys (she pointed at one row of soldiers), put down your brushes and go and collect all the pots of turquoise paint and bring them here. The next three, go and find a large container—something like a washing tub—and the rest of you, over there, go and find as many sieves as you can. Then you can all get to work pouring the paint into the tub through the sieves. I shall recommend full military honours for the one who finds the key."

On hearing about possible military honours, twenty-three Colorwally soldiers eagerly ran off in different directions to carry out the girl's instructions.

"Brilliant," muttered Sheriff Tomato. "Quite brilliant!"

Rachel had never before seen folk work so quickly. All the pots of turquoise paint were lined up in front of her and their lids prized open. Working in pairs, the Colorwally troops began to pour paint from the pots through the sieves into a tub. Quite soon there was a shriek of delight from a bearded, emerald green Colorwally.

"The key, Advisor Rachel! I've found the key. Look!"

The excited man held up a large red key above his head and did a little dance. His resemblance to an Irish leprechaun made the girl chuckle to herself.

"Awesome!" exclaimed the sheriff. "Full military honours for you," he added before taking the key from the soldier and wiping it on his uniform.

Rachel was led to a door at the far end of the hall. The sheriff opened the door and stepped back to allow the girl to enter.

"Our secret weapon... the paint tank!" Sheriff Tomato

proudly announced. "This'll take those Dullabillies by surprise."

Rachel stared in wonder at the most extraordinary contraption she had ever seen. Like a giant fish tank on legs, four jointed limbs with large red saucepan-lid feet pointing towards the door, the secret weapon appeared ready to start marching off to war that very moment. She saw that it held several containers brimming with paints of different colours. From these protruded long, blue tubes, of which one end dangled in the paint whilst the other was capped with a revolving nozzle. The tubes resembled periscopes, and on one side of the tank was a display of buttons and dials. Rachel reckoned these were to control the tank's walking plus direct the paint from the nozzles at intended targets. What a wonderfully mucky mess it would make, she thought.

"Inventor Lemon's latest war machine!" explained the sheriff, observing Rachel's interest.

"Lemon?"

Rachel had visions of a Colorwally whose face was an even brighter yellow than that of President Banana, and she tried again not to giggle.

"Yes, Lemon. Trouble is, he's gone on holiday to the Costa Amarilla and no one here knows the code number to get the thing to start. We think he gave it to General Greengage, but there's no way of knowing. The general's far too preoccupied sorting out his brushes to help us with the matter." Sheriff Tomato blinked a few times and Rachel *did* giggle. "And then *you* worked it out. Just like that. A miracle!"

Rachel stopped giggling and looked at the sheriff. She felt uneasy.

"Hold on a second. You mean that number I mentioned when I was... um... doing long division?"

"Precisely! What a clever military advisor, I told myself. She's worked out the code number for the secret weapon by doing long division."

"Wait a minute, I didn't—"

"This is no time for modesty, please, Advisor Rachel. I can see why they said they were sending us the greatest military advisor of all time."

Rachel reckoned that if she were to tell the little man the truth now, he would just blink himself crazy.

"Sergeant!" the sheriff called out. Sergeant Lobster, who was busy polishing the paint tank with a lobster-red cloth, glanced up.

"Sheriff Tomato, sir!"

"Key in the number eleven point two seven, please."

Rachel's heart sank as the sergeant tapped at keys and 11.27 appeared on a screen. Nothing happened.

I knew it, she thought.

Sheriff Tomato began to blink again. He looked pleadingly at the girl who now felt bad. Although she had no intention of going to war the following day, she still did not like to see the sheriff get upset and possibly lose his job.

"It's got to be the right number if Advisor Rachel gave it to us," the distressed little fellow insisted. "Isn't there something else you could try?"

"What about the instruction manual?" Rachel asked. "When my daddy gets anything electrical from Amazon it always comes with an instruction manual."

"Guess that might have been the paper we saw General Greengage painting on. Probably testing out his brushes. If there'd been any instructions there they'd now be totally covered with red paint."

Sheriff Tomato looked thoroughly miserable. Under his anxious gaze, Rachel went up to the paint tank and carefully examined all the knobs and dials and buttons. She spied a little switch the same colour as the rest of the tank in one of the corners. She flicked this up. The tank leapt into the air and started to run backwards. It crashed into the wall, splashing paint all over the place. Fortunately, the wall was strong, otherwise the awesome machine might have broken through and escaped. Its feet angrily pounded away as it continued to run against the obstruction of a wall, the red metal shoes making a scraping sound as they slid over the painted concrete. Rachel rushed forward to switch the thing off.

The tank stopped with one foot raised above the ground, ready for its next step backwards. The girl carefully studied the controls. There was a lever that could move either forwards or backwards. It had been set in the backwards position. Beside this was a dial. To one side of the dial was the word 'fast', at the other end 'slow'. She slid the lever forwards and turned the dial to 'slow'. Anxiously biting her lower lip, she switched the machine on, again. The foot suspended in the air hit the ground with a bang, then, in slow motion, the tank began to walk sedately away from the wall. When back in its former position, Rachel turned the machine off and grinned at Sheriff Tomato. He was smiling from one red ear to the other. It was the second time she had seen him smile and it made her positively glow inside. Her daddy would have been really proud of her if he knew that she had fixed a secret, though harmless, weapon.

"Awesome!" the sheriff exclaimed, clapping his hands with glee. "So, we're all set for the big battle. I'm convinced your strategy will work. We *shall* be victorious tomorrow, without a shadow of doubt."

Rachel really did not want to think about the tomorrow bit. Even if they had no guns, grenades or shells, it could still get nasty, particularly if the Dullabillies and Colorwallies were to fight with fists like some of the boys at school. Alec never fought, though. Rachel only ever thought of him as a quiet, shy boy who always came top in all subjects. Not the son of a couple of witches. In fact, she *almost* quite liked Alec, though would never dare tell this to anyone. If Alec was on the other side—and she was certain that the boy she had seen walking down the grey path towards Dullabillieville had been him—then perhaps they might get a chance to meet up during the battle and arrange a treaty. She had learned about treaties from her history teacher at school.

"I think I should get back to Mrs Pink now to check on my assistant," Rachel told the sheriff. She was missing Waffles and was also beginning to feel hungry, particularly knowing that Mrs Pink was such a good cook.

"Assistant Waffles? Quite!" the man agreed. "We must

hurry, because," he added.

"Because of what?" Rachel grinned. He was such a strange little person.

"Because of the fact that..."

"That I need to check on Waffles?" Rachel suggested.

"Precisely. Hit the nail on the head, Advisor Rachel. The *nail* on the *head!*"

So off they ran in the direction of Mrs Pink's pink cottage along the brightly decorated streets of Colorwallytown. Even running on the level caused the sheriff to pant, and Rachel thought they should slow down. In fact, she wondered why he always felt he had to run everywhere when he was so bad at running. She did not wish him to feel he had to keep up with her. After all, she was an exceptionally fast runner.

"I think we could slow down a little," she suggested on hearing the sheriff mumble, "Oh dear, oh dear, they really should make *all* roads go downhill all the time."

"I'm sure Waffles will be all right with Mrs Pink," Rachel added, "so there's no need to hurry," and they slowed to a more leisurely trot.

"I was such a good runner as a young Tomato," Sheriff Tomato informed the girl just before reaching the pink cottage. "Nearly as fast as a Greengage." Luckily, he did not hear the girl giggle, and he seemed so pleased with the fact. "You know, sadly the annual running competition is now always won by a Greengage."

Control yourself, Rachel, a voice in the girl's head warned as she snorted into her cupped hand.

Chapter 8

Rachel was so relieved to be back inside the cottage after bidding Sheriff Tomato a giggling goodnight. He had bowed almost to the ground and informed her he would be back in the morning at seven fifty-nine sharp. When she questioned him, "Why not eight o'clock?" he just blinked frantically, so she hurriedly agreed to be ready at seven fifty-nine.

"Is Waffles okay?" she asked Mrs Pink.

"Sleeping blissfully," the woman assured her. "I've been checking on him every few minutes. By the way, does he snore?"

"Well, he sometimes makes a sort of hamsterish noise when he's asleep. I suppose it's when he's dreaming."

"Oh! What does he dream about?"

"I expect he was dreaming about your lovely cake," Rachel replied.

Her nose was tempted by delicious cooking smells as thoughts of food entered her head.

"Your supper's ready for you when you've washed your hands, my dear."

Standing in her private, en-suite bathroom, Rachel

thought it so unfair she always had to wash her hands before eating and Waffles didn't, but then she reckoned that hamsters perhaps have stronger stomachs than people.

What an amazing meal! Shepherd's pie, her all-time favourite, with the yummiest of vegetables. Rachel was given a glass of blueberry and mango juice and found it so difficult to know whether she preferred the blueberry or the mango taste that she simply had to ask for another glassful to help her come to a decision... and still she couldn't!

"Well, my dear, you'll just have to have more for breakfast before deciding," laughed Mrs Pink.

Then there was the dessert. A chocolate mousse with a pink meringue and red fruit sauce, and she didn't even have to ask for another helping. Mrs Pink seemed to know it was what she wished for from the expression on her face.

That night, Rachel felt strangely happy as she snuggled down between the warm pink sheets listening to the sniffly, sleepy sounds coming from her military assistant. No one would ever believe her back home, nor her friends at school, if she were to tell them she had been a military advisor in a war, although perhaps Alec might. She now truly hoped she *would* meet up with him the following day, regardless of her pink hair. Mostly to arrange a treaty. Also, she was determined to find out whether or not there was any truth in the story about his parents being witches. If they weren't witches, she was sure going to give those mean kids at school a darn good telling off.

Rachel was not too worried that her mommy might be

missing her. Something inside her said everything would be just fine back in Houston, and that when she got home her mommy wouldn't have even noticed that she'd been gone.

"Wake up, my dear," said a gentle voice.

Rachel opened her eyes. For a brief moment she wondered where on earth she was. Then it all came back. Pink hair, big smile... Mrs Pink! She turned her head and saw that her own hair was pink and there, with his pink head poking above the pink sheet, was her hamster, Waffles, his eyes still closed.

"Wake up, Waffles," she said, giving him a gentle prod. He opened his eyes and twitched his nose. "It's our big day. I'm relying on you to help me with my strategy, you know."

"Best strategy is to sue for peace, Advisor Rachel," suggested Mrs Pink.

"Sue?" asked Rachel, sitting up. "I thought you only sued people who did mean things to you."

"Well, war *is* mean. Come, your breakfast's ready. Better eat up before the sheriff gets here. Mustn't keep him waiting."

"Think it'll make him blink if I do?" Rachel asked cheekily. Mrs Pink laughed.

"So much he won't be able to see you," the woman agreed. "Can't have that, can we?"

As Rachel slipped into her pink dress, placing Waffles in her pocket, she could not help but think that Mrs Pink was the only Colorwally with whom she could share a joke.

The breakfast was as delicious as the supper had been the previous night. First, an amazing pink cereal that Mrs Pink said was made from a special pink fruit, the name of which Rachel had never heard of, and it tasted better than anything she could possibly imagine... and she was particularly keen on fruit. Next, humungous sausages and the most wonderful scrambled egg ever created, followed by toast and pink jelly, the jelly made from that same pink fruit. Finally, she enjoyed another large glass of blueberry and mango juice and still could not decide which of the two flavours she preferred.

"Well, you'll just have to come back one day and have more, won't you, my dear?" said Mrs Pink, smiling. "Must get it right, ay?"

"I'd just love to come back. And so would... oh dear!" the girl exclaimed. "I forgot all about Waffles. He must be starving!"

Guiltily, she extracted the snuffling little pink golden hamster from her dress pocket.

"That's quite all right, my dear," said Mrs Pink, placing a doll-sized plate on the table, with morsels of everything that Rachel had just eaten. "His breakfast's all ready. See!"

"Oh, thank you, Mrs Pink."

Rachel carefully placed Waffles beside his plate and watched as he filled his pouches before lapping up blueberry and mango juice from a thimble. When he looked up at Rachel again, his nose was golden once again.

"Hey!" exclaimed the girl. "The dye's come off his nose. He does look weird."

"Quick!" fussed Mrs Pink. "Brush your teeth now. The

sheriff will be here in three minutes!"

Rachel hurried to the bathroom, envious of Waffles who did not have to bother with such things as the brushing of teeth, and got back just in time to hear a frenzied knock at the front door. She quickly returned her hamster to his hiding place in her dress. Before opening the door, Mrs Pink slipped a piece of paper into her hand.

"If you see him—Mr Whitestone—please give him this note," the woman whispered. Rachel pulled open her dress pocket, popped in the note, and spoke severely to Waffles:

"Now don't you go eating Mrs Pink's note!" she warned. Despite his pouches being full, she was not one hundred percent certain it would be safe.

"No time to lose, no time to lose!" insisted Sheriff Tomato as soon as Mr Pink opened the door. His face was even redder. "We must hurry!"

Perhaps he's put on special red war paint, thought the girl. She had read about Native American tribes using war paint and had often wondered why they did that. There again, she could never understand why people wanted to go to war anyway.

Chapter 9

As Sheriff Tomato and Rachel hastened along the colourful street, the girl felt cross for not being allowed time to give Mrs Pink a proper hug. Whatever happened, that would be her first priority after the war was over.

The streets were now lined by women and children cheering and waving multi-coloured flags as she ran past, and this softened her anger. After Sheriff Tomato explained they were cheering her, because the whole town had been talking about their brilliant new military advisor—Advisor Rachel—her face positively shone.

When they arrived at the arsenal, the troops were already lined up in neat rows, brushes and paint pots at the ready, whilst Sergeant Lobster was standing stiff with pride beside the paint tank. The entire Colorwally army bowed with military precision as Rachel entered. That is, all bar a thin, bent little green Colorwally who stood alone at the back clutching a bright red brush. General Greengage.

"You wish to inspect the troops, Advisor Rachel?" queried the sergeant.

Rachel could not refuse, so once again she walked up

and down before the lines of soldiers, smiling like a princess. She found it frustrating that no one smiled back at her, but then she supposed people weren't meant to smile when they were about to go off to war. She bowed to General Greengage because she thought that bowing to a general was right and proper, but all he did was to wave his brush at her. Sergeant Lobster reassured Rachel that the paint tank had been tested earlier that morning and was fully operational. Then Sheriff Tomato asked Rachel whether her strategy was "the same as?"

"Same as what?" she asked.

"As was," he answered.

"Was what?"

"Going round."

"Where?"

"Inside!"

"Inside what?"

"Where!"

"Where?"

"Where it's going round."

Rachel, who was by now getting used to Sheriff Tomato, gave up and said "yes" and he seemed happy with that.

The sheriff peered at his watch and started to count backwards "ten, nine, eight..." Rachel glanced at her own watch. The minute hand was almost at twenty-four minutes past the hour. "Seven, six, five, four, three, two, one... WE'RE AT WAR!" he screeched.

Off they marched, the sheriff and Rachel, with Waffles in her dress pocket, in the lead, closely followed by the multi-coloured Colorwally troops, after which trotted the zany paint tank on its red-shoed feet. Sergeant Lobster, who marched along beside it, was randomly turning dials and twiddling knobs on the control panel. General Greengage followed up in the rear, quite content with his brushes.

What an odd army we must look, thought Rachel as they marched along streets lined by yelling, painted children and applauding, painted moms. The girl considered it strange that there didn't seem to be any old people around apart from General Greengage who was obviously no youngster, but then she reckoned that if their white hair had been dyed and the wrinkles painted over, perhaps they might not appear old.

When the Colorwally army reached the coloured bridge, Rachel looked across the river at the black, grey and white town of Dullabillieville, its austere buildings starkly reflected in the still, blue-grey water of the river. She had to admit it looked a dull place, particularly without any people around, but she did not think dullness was a good reason for going to war, and she seriously doubted whether there were any witches on either side of the river. She was just about to say to Sheriff Tomato that perhaps they should all go home because there was nobody about in Dullabillieville, and that witches were only a figment of people's imaginations, when the sheriff turned to face the troops, raised his right hand and shouted in a commanding voice without a single blink:

"Across the bridge, quick march!"

Too late! They were at war. She now prayed that she

might quickly meet up with Alec and together they could call a truce.

When the army reached the quiet, dull grey riverfront of Dullabillieville, Sheriff Tomato seemed over the moon. "At long last," he said to the girl. "Thank you for making this possible, Advisor Rachel."

Rachel did not think she had anything to do with them being there. She watched with mounting trepidation whilst the troops marched off the bridge and formed themselves into neat little units of colourful soldiers, ten per unit. As she observed them remove lids from paint-pots in unison and stir the paint with their brushes, her attention was diverted by a loud, clunking noise. The paint tank was walking off the bridge on its metallic shoes. Sergeant Lobster brought the cumbersome contraption to a halt by flicking the switch. He poked at buttons and twiddled knobs. Periscope nozzles, sticking up from the containers of paint, began to twist and bend in response, and the thing looked more like a giant child's toy than a weapon of war. Rachel glanced back at General Greengage who remained on the bridge where he was busy dabbing at something with a blue brush.

"Battle formation at the ready!" yelled Sheriff Tomato. Rachel wondered how a little person like that could make such a big noise. "Battle commence!" he shouted, going an even deeper shade of red.

"Thank goodness there are no Dullabillies around," Rachel whispered to Waffles. She knew he would be terrified if there was any actual fighting. Admittedly, the Colorwallies were small—none were over five feet tall—but even small people hitting each other would be frightening for a little hamster.

Chapter 10

Rachel stood timidly beside Sheriff Tomato as each unit of soldiers crossed the street in formation. They were well-organised. Attacking alternate Dullabillie houses, they painted with surprising speed, sloshing great daubs of red, purple, orange, green—whatever the colours of paint in their pots happened to be—over the first floor walls, doors and window frames. Then other members of their units climbed up onto the shoulders of the first wave of soldiers and began to paint higher up. After that—and this was quite something—a third wave of Colorwallies climbed up onto the shoulders of these soldiers and, using paint sprayers, started to spray the dull, grey roofs bright, gaudy colours. Rachel giggled when it occurred to her that they resembled circus clowns doing acrobatics.

"Oh dear, not another caterpillar, I hope?" asked Sheriff Tomato, glancing anxiously at the girl.

"No, no," reassured Rachel. "It's Waffles this time. He does tickle."

"Thank goodness, thank goodness," the little man muttered, turning his attention again to the ongoing battle. When he was reasonably happy that every other

Dullabillieville riverfront house was a nice bright colour, the sheriff shouted to Sergeant Lobster, who was still fiddling with buttons and dials on the paint tank.

"Paint tank at the ready!" he screamed. Rachel covered her ears and worried about Waffles' ears.

"Sir!" came the equally loud reply.

"Paint tank forward!"

Sergeant Lobster flicked a switch. The tank did a little skip, splashing plops of paint, before clanking forwards.

"Stand back, Advisor Rachel!" warned Sheriff Tomato.

Together they stood flat against the grey wall flanking the river whilst the paint tank trundled past on its red metal feet. Rachel soon discovered why the sheriff got her to stand back, for paint flew in all directions from the tank's revolving nozzles. It made a terrible mess of the sidewalk and road as it ambled along the riverfront, turning Sergeant Lobster variously yellow, pink, green, and blue whilst spraying anything and everything within range. Rachel had another burst of giggles because she had once heard that lobsters change colour when being cooked, although probably not quite the strange mix of colours covering the sergeant. *Perhaps he should be renamed Sergeant Rainbow*, she thought, *like the carousel animal.*

Close by, Rachel heard childish shrieks of delight. Two young children, about five and seven, ran from one of the buildings. Somehow they had managed to get hold of two brushes and pots of paint which they started to splash over each other. The two Colorwally soldiers whose paints and brushes the children had found looked sheepishly at Sheriff Tomato and shrugged their shoulders.

"Oh dear, what a waste of valuable paint!" the Sheriff said.

Rachel did not like to say the whole war was an appalling waste of paint. Anyway, she was more concerned that the children should come to no harm.

"Please make sure no one hurts the children," she begged Sheriff Tomato. "I'm going over to them."

The sheriff shouted to the soldiers who had lost their brushes:

"Troops, leave all the prisoners to Advisor Rachel!"

All the prisoners? Rachel looked up and down the Dullabillieville riverfront, and still only saw two young children who were having a whale of a time. She walked over to them, leaving the sheriff standing by himself and wittering on about the shocking price of paint.

"Hello," Rachel said. "Are you enjoying yourselves?"

"Yeah!" replied the little girl, the younger of the two. "This is great. We're never normally allowed to play with anything that's coloured. But our Daddy does take us across the river sometimes. To get colourful toys."

"Shhh!" warned the boy putting his finger to his lips. "We're not supposed to say. Remember? Daddy says it's called smuggling. It's all right if it makes us happy, but no one else must know."

"Oh!" exclaimed the girl.

She had a white-painted face, hands and legs, and a white dress and shoes, now dappled red and yellow. The boy, even more splashed with red and yellow, had a black face with black clothes.

Rachel remembered. Could these children be

Snowdrop and Nerino? She looked inside her dress pocket for that piece of paper with the message from Mrs Pink to Mr Whitestone. Waffles must have nibbled at it.

"Oh, you bad little hamster!" the girl reprimanded. Fortunately, he had only taken away the edges, so she could still read what was written:

'*Dear Mr Whitestone,*
If you need any help with the washing of clothes or the cooking of meals or the looking after of children, please let me know. It would afford me very great pleasure to be of assistance to you.
Yours very sincerely,
Mrs Pink.'

Rachel turned it over, and on the back was a carefully drawn map which showed Mr Whitestone how to find the pink cottage. She looked up at the children who had resumed their game of paint splashing.

"Are you Nerino?" she asked the boy.

"Sure am!" he laughed. He ran behind Rachel to dodge his sister who was coming at him with a brush dripping with red paint.

"And you're Snowdrop?" she asked the little girl.

"Yeah!" the child replied, reaching behind Rachel with her brush.

"Wait, children, wait!" begged Rachel. "If you're very good you might get more coloured toys."

Immediately, the children stopped playing and stood attentively in front of the older girl. She showed Nerino the message.

"Can you read?" she asked.

"Of course I can," he protested. "My daddy taught me. *And* he gets those books with coloured pictures from the other side of the river. I'm reading one about a little tiger. They've got yellow stripes, you know."

"Well..." continued Rachel, "this is a very important message for a gentleman called Mr Whitestone."

Snowdrop snatched the letter and jumped up and down with excitement.

"That's my daddy, that's my daddy!" she sang. "Can I give it to him?"

"No, I'll give it," insisted Nerino, grabbing the letter from Rachel. "Because I'm older."

"That's not fair," complained Snowdrop, stomping her foot and trying to take the letter back from her brother.

"Hey, you guys!" exclaimed Rachel. "If you two stay friends then you can say 'hello' to Waffles."

Chapter 11

The two children stopped squabbling and stared at Rachel.

"Who's Waffles?" asked Snowdrop. Her expression informed the older girl that whoever Waffles was, he had to be a very important person to say 'hello' to.

"He's my pet golden hamster. But at the moment he's pink. Apart from his nose."

"Let me see him, let me see!" Snowdrop shrieked, hopping from one foot to the other.

"And *me*!" insisted Nerino.

"Only if you're going to be good friends," warned Rachel, her face deadly serious. Perhaps too serious, for Snowdrop looked uneasy.

"Ask my daddy," she said. "He'll tell you we're good friends."

"Hold out your hands," Rachel instructed. "Both of you."

The Dullabillie children dropped their brushes and held out their hands. Rachel reached into her dress pocket and lifted out Waffles, placing him in Snowdrop's cupped palms. The child's eyes widened.

"Does he talk?" she asked as Waffles peered up at her

and twitched his nose.

"No, but he understands when you talk to him," Rachel replied. "At least, I think he does."

"Can he sing?" questioned Snowdrop. "I love singing."

"No! But he's good at snoring."

"I can't snore," the little girl said. "Not when I'm awake, anyway."

Nerino stroked Waffles and the hamster clearly enjoyed being the centre of attention.

"Will you hold him now, please?" Snowdrop asked her brother. "So that I can stroke him?"

And so Waffles got passed backwards and forwards between the two children as they took turns in holding and stroking him until Rachel worried that he might get dizzy and vomit. She retrieved her hamster and put him back in her pocket.

"What's *your* name?" Nerino asked.

"Just Rachel," she answered. She much preferred 'Rachel' to 'Advisor Rachel'.

"Are you a Colorwally?"

"No. I'm an ordinary schoolgirl from Houston."

"Where's that?"

"Texas."

"Where's that?"

"The United States of America."

"Where's that?"

Rachel was about to say, 'the universe', but instead explained that it was a big country with a red, white and blue flag. She found it difficult to work out where this strange world of Colorwallytown and Dullabillieville was in the universe that she knew back home. She could not imagine anywhere else in her own world where even small children had not heard of America or of hamsters.

"Now you will be careful with that important message for your daddy, won't you?" she asked Snowdrop and Nerino, having seen the piece of paper pass backwards and forwards between brother and sister.

"Of course we will! We'd like to ask you to come inside our house, Rachel," Nerino said, "but Daddy's gone to war and left us alone with Granny and she's always grumpy in the mornings. She's better in the afternoons because she's usually asleep."

Rachel told them they should perhaps go indoors and wash the paint off before their daddy came home.

"Can I wash *all* the paint off?" Snowdrop asked. "The white stuff as well. I'd much prefer to be pink like you, but..." She paused and studied Rachel in a critical sort of way. "But perhaps not my hair," she added. "What colour's your *real* hair? Mine's yellow."

"That's so funny, isn't it?" said Rachel. "Because mine's black!"

"Are we on the wrong sides then?" asked Nerino. "My real hair's yellow too. Our mom had yellow hair."

"There shouldn't have to be sides," replied Rachel. She looked around to make sure no Colorwallies were within earshot. "I think this war is very silly," she added in a whisper.

"That's exactly what Daddy said this morning," Nerino told her.

"Will we see you again?" asked Snowdrop.

"I hope so," replied Rachel, "but if you pass the message on to your daddy, I'm sure you'll get to see Mrs Pink some time. And she makes awesome cakes!"

Rachel gave both Snowdrop and Nerino a hug and watched as they dawdled back towards their Dullabillieville home.

"I do hope Daddy gets back soon 'cos I love cake," she overheard Snowdrop say to her brother, so she felt confident that the message would be delivered.

The girl rejoined Sheriff Tomato beside the river and was about to tell him she had released the prisoners as an act of compassion when she noticed the little man had frozen like a lump of stone, his face distorted in horror. Looking across the river at Colorwallytown, she saw why. Whilst the Colorwallies had been happily painting every other Dullabillieville riverfront house bright colours, without any resistance from the enemy, the Dullabillie army was over there on the other side of the river doing exactly the same thing to the riverfront houses of Colorwallytown with black, white and grey paint.

Rachel would have been hard pressed to tell the difference between the riverfronts of the two towns, with every other house either coloured or black/white/grey on both sides of the river. To add to Sheriff Tomato's distress, a secret weapon, identical to their own, was spraying grey paint all over the beautiful coloured road and sidewalk of his lovely hometown. The poor sheriff seemed to be in state of shock. He began to blink so fast Rachel had difficulty making out his eyes. He kept on muttering, "Terrible, terrible!" and "What will the President say, what *will* he say?" The girl saw, in the distance, the golden palace tower peeping above the houses of Colorwallytown, and on its balcony, a yellow and a violet blob. Doubtless the President and the First Lady were overseeing the war through binoculars.

"Don't worry, Sheriff Tomato. I have a strategy," she reassured the funny little man. "Wait here and ask Sergeant Lobster to switch off the paint tank. That's a very important part of my strategy."

"Strategy? What, what?" the sheriff asked, so upset he did not appear to be listening properly. Rachel patted him on the back to comfort him.

"It's okay," she insisted. "Everything will be fine. Leave it all to me. Just get your sergeant to turn off the paint tank and ask our troops to stop awhile and clean up their brushes. Tell them they'll all be getting medals. And you, Sheriff Tomato, will have a special decoration for outstanding bravery. I'll tell the President myself!"

She had heard about soldiers being decorated and had always wondered whether decorating a soldier was a bit like decorating a Christmas tree. She could ask Mrs Pink if she had any Christmas baubles or fairy lights to hang on the sheriff.

"Me a decorated Tomato?" questioned the sheriff.

Please don't giggle, Rachel, the girl silently begged herself as she tried to empty her mind of thoughts of a large, happy tomato with fancy lights and coloured baubles hanging from it.

"Wait here whilst I carry out my strategy," she quickly said. Then, "Everything's going to be all right now,

Waffles," she told her hamster as she headed back over the bridge towards Colorwallytown where the Dullabillies were still gaily splashing black, white and grey paint all over the place. "I know what I'm doing."

Rachel met General Greengage on the bridge. He had laid out his brushes in a neat row along the wall and was deeply engrossed in moving them around. The look on his face suggested this was the most important thing that anyone had ever done.

"General Greengage!" Rachel called out, saluting as she had seen people do in movies.

"Yes, that's me," affirmed the little fellow. "Commander of the Colorwally army, you know."

"Yes, I do know. And I've come to tell you the war's over."

"What war?" he asked.

"The one against the Dullabillies," the girl replied.

"The who?"

"Yes," she said. It seemed a whole lot easier to say "yes" rather than try to explain, and the general seemed perfectly happy with this.

Rachel ran on over the bridge towards Colorwallytown. On reaching the other side, she breathed a sigh of relief. There, looking as silly as she felt, stood Alec with a bunch of black and white Dullabillies.

"Alec!" she cried out, over the moon at seeing him.

He appeared surprised and stared at her as if wondering who this pink person calling his name might be.

"Alec!" she shouted again, more loudly. "It's me! Rachel! From school!"

The boy appeared embarrassed. A good sign, Rachel reckoned, and she knew why he felt so awkward. His normally pink face had been painted as black as pitch, and he seemed to be wondering whether or not to make a run for it.

"It's okay, Alec," she continued, lowering her voice. "My hair looks silly, anyway. I'll not tell at school about your face, honest, if you don't let on about my pink hair. Please, we have to talk. Like urgently."

Alec politely excused himself from the Dullabillies who were so wrapped up in discussing the war that they had not noticed Rachel with her pink hair and pink dress. He ran over to where the girl stood at the end of the bridge.

"What are you doing here, Rachel?" he asked. "And why *is* your hair all pink?"

Chapter 12

"Well... it was like this," began Rachel.

"I got on the carousel in the mall back home and ended up on a purple hill. There I met a funny little red man called 'Sheriff Tomato who told me I was his Military Advisor and he brought me here to Colorwallytown," she continued. "I had no choice. Apparently he thought I was their military advisor and took me to a Mrs Pink who dyed my hair pink before I was allowed to see the President. Oh, and Waffles got dyed pink too."

"Waffles?"

"He's my pet golden hamster! Look!"

Rachel showed Waffles to Alec.

"Wow, I've never seen a pink golden hamster before," the boy said, chuckling.

"Well, I'm going to wash him as soon as I get back to Mrs Pink's place. *And* my hair! I hate having pink hair."

"And I hate looking like a coal miner!" Alec complained.

Rachel grinned, for she felt totally relaxed with the boy. If he had really been the son of a couple of witches, he would have been completely different, she was sure of it.

"You could wash your face at Mrs Pink's as well. She's really nice. And you should try her scrumptious cake," the girl said. "But look, I've a plan. I call it my strategy."

"Yeah, they keep asking me for *my* strategy. Not sure what they're talking about. Particularly Sheriff Nightsky. Just makes me laugh most of the time."

"Sounds a bit like Sheriff Tomato," observed Rachel.

"But I kind of like Lieutenant Whitestone. He's—"

"Whitestone? Where is he? I met his children. They're really cute," exclaimed Rachel.

"Over there," replied Alec, pointing to a tall man with a white face, white hair, bright, twinkling eyes and a long, white cloak. "He says this war business is stupid. And you know what? He told me he secretly changed the order he gave for all the paint they've been using from water-resistant to water washable. The others don't know this, but the paint will easily wash off when it next rains. He reckons you lot might not want half your houses painted black and grey by his troops. 'They should be allowed to make their own choice,' he said. I promised him not to tell anyone, but it's okay to tell you because you're enemy."

Rachel frowned.

"I don't *feel* like enemy," she objected.

"Sorry! Anyway, you're not *my* enemy. Only theirs. And another thing," Alec continued, "his secret contact on the Colorwally side was going do the same with *their* paint."

"Thank goodness," Rachel said, thinking of Snowdrop and Nerino covered in red and yellow paint. She hoped their grumpy granny would not give them too hard a time.

"So, what's your strategy then?" asked Alec.

"Well, when I saw Sheriff Tomato getting so worked up at seeing the Dullabillies in Colorwallytown doing exactly what his soldiers were doing in Dullabillieville, I got worried the two armies might actually meet up and really fight. That would upset Waffles because he just hates fighting," the girl explained. "So I thought we should arrange a treaty."

"Sounds good to me," agreed Alec. "But how do we do that? I already suggested the same thing to General Black but he said we couldn't have one as he's lost his dictionary and can't look up the word 'treaty'. He's as dotty as a ladybug."

"Bit like General Greengage," said Rachel. "All *he* does is play with his brushes and I don't think he even realises we're at war. Anyway, we'll need a piece of paper. I can get that from Mrs Pink. And we should write at the top of the page in posh writing, 'The Treaty of... erm...'" Rachel paused. "What should we call our treaty, Alec?" she asked.

Alec looked pensive before his face suddenly lit up.

"The Treaty of Waffles?"

"Yeah!" exclaimed Rachel. "I like it! The Treaty of Waffles! Because he's a peace loving hamster. We'll get our generals to sign it. They probably won't have a clue what they're signing, anyway. We must sign as well, of course. And... well, do you think the presidents should sign?"

"Certainly! Wouldn't be valid if they didn't. And it might help to make them feel important."

"Huh! Can say that again. Them feeling important's what this is all about, I reckon," declared Rachel. "Hey...

I've an idea. How about holding a tea-party on the bridge here? We'll invite the presidents and I'll go get Mrs Pink to bring along the rest of her cake. Other stuff as well. Plus cups and plates. And we'll tell the presidents they can have some of her cake as soon as they've signed our treaty."

"Brilliant, Rachel!"

"That's what the President kept saying when I met him yesterday," she told the boy. Her face felt hot and red, for the way Alec said 'brilliant' seemed so different from when the sheriff and the President used the same word. It was as though he really meant it. "Another thing…" she continued, "I think Mrs Pink wants to meet your Lieutenant Whitestone. We must make sure that he gets some of her cake."

"So, what now, Advisor Rachel?" asked Alec.

Rachel laughed.

"Well, Advisor Alec, you could kind of ask your troops to stop painting. Politely, of course. Tell them they need a rest. My daddy calls it his coffee break, only we don't have any coffee here."

"I guess Lieutenant Whitestone will be only too pleased to get them to stop."

"Then we can go round to Mrs Pink's and tell her about the tea-party on the bridge. And then…" Rachel paused.

"The presidents?"

"Mmm!"

For a few moments, the children stood in silent thought.

"Got it," Rachel said at last. "Each of us goes to our own president as his military advisor and invites him to a tea party to mark the end of the war. We don't have to say nobody won. Each will reckon his own side won, anyway. Then we'll take them to the party, show them the cake and just say they can have some as soon as they've signed the Treaty of Waffles."

"Won't Waffles have to sign too?" Alec asked.

"Of course. He can make a paw print," suggested Rachel. "There's plenty of paint around for him to do that."

"So, Advisor Rachel... agreed?"

Alec held up his right hand.

"Agreed, Advisor Alec!" affirmed Rachel, high fiving with the boy. "By the way," she asked, "do you believe in witches?"

"Rubbish, all that stuff. Why?"

"Oh, nothing! Now go and tell Lieutenant Whitestone the war's over. He's by himself."

Alec went and told Lieutenant Whitestone to command the Dullabillie troops to have a 'coffee break without coffee', then he and Rachel ran off together in the direction of Mrs Pink's house. Away from the riverfront, crowds cheered when the kids shouted out "The war is over!" No one showed the least concern that Alec had a black painted face. Mrs Pink was over the moon to see Rachel again and delighted to meet Alec. Rachel decided the woman must have read her mind because she had already baked another cake and had a large pot of tea ready, "...In case of celebrations."

"I think Alec wants to wash his face first," Rachel announced. "And I really would like to make my hair black again, Mrs Pink."

"Oh!" replied the woman. "We have a problem. You see, it's too soon to wash out the dye. You'll have to wait at least a month."

Rachel's heart sank like a stone. The thought of going to school the following day with pink hair filled her with dread.

"You could shave it off and wear a wig," suggested Alec, trying to be helpful, but this only made Rachel cross.

"That's not funny, Alec!" she snapped. "In fact, it's really dumb!"

Chapter 13

Alec looked truly sheepish as Rachel picked up Waffles and stroked his nose. She often did that at home if someone made her feel cross. Suddenly she realised that Waffles' nose was no longer pink because he'd put it in the blueberry and mango juice. The dye had come off. Her face lit up.

"Could you spare some blueberry and mango juice for my hair?" she asked.

"Now why would you want to put juice on your hair?" responded the woman, baffled.

"It'll come off. See? Waffles' nose is his normal colour, golden, because he dipped it in the blueberry and mango juice. The same should happen with my hair. The dye'll come out. I'm sure of it."

It worked. When Alec returned with a pink face, having washed off the black paint, he found Rachel had black hair again. It was all sticky so she had to go and wash it with shampoo and water. She also cleaned her pink shoes with blueberry and mango juice. It almost felt strange to wear white shoes again. After this, they set to work on Waffles, dipping him, nose up, into a jug of blueberry and mango juice, then gently rubbing him until he was once more a lovely golden brown colour. When he was dried and safely back in Rachel's dress pocket, the two children sat down to prepare the Treaty of Waffles. Alec wrote it out because he had neater writing. Rachel felt certain this meant he was not truly a nerd because nerds and geeks, like professors, would surely have scrawly writing.

Rachel dictated the words of the treaty:

'*We hereby declare a State of Peace between Colorwallytown and Dullabillieville. A person may wear what he or she likes in either town and have his or her face any colour or black or white and paint brushes should only be used for peaceful purposes. After signing this Treaty, each of the Presidents may have his cake and eat it.*'

Alec paused. "Do we need to put that in?" he asked. "About eating cake?"

"Definitely!" replied Rachel crossly, feeling offended to think that Alec would wish to exclude anything she dictated. She had once overheard her daddy say, "*So-and-so* wants to have his cake and eat it," and assumed it must be important.

Alec continued to prepare the Treaty of Waffles:

The Treaty of Waffles

We hereby declare a State of Peace between Colorwallytown and Dullabillieville. A person may wear what he or she pleases in either town and have his or her face any color they wish, or aclok or white, and paint brushes must only be used for peaceful purposes.

After signing this treaty, each of the two presidents may have his cake and eat it.

Signed:

....(President of Colorwallytown)

....(President of Dullabillieville)

....(Colorwally Military Advisor)

....(Dullabillie Military Advisor)

(Waffles' Paw Print)

Date:

............/............/............

Together, Rachel and Alec gazed with shared pride at the treaty. They gave it to Mrs Pink to take down to the bridge, together with a pot of tea and the cake. She said she would get friends to bring along more tea, cookies, cupcakes, plates and cups, and the three went off in separate directions, Rachel to the palace to invite President Banana and First Lady Violet, and Alec to do the same with President Coalface and First Lady Snow White. He would also stop off on the way to tell Lieutenant Whitestone about the new strategy. Mrs Pink was to inform Sheriff Tomato and General Greengage, and then get things ready for the tea party on the bridge.

Chapter 14

Rachel felt both important and excited as she approached the Grand Palace of Colorwallytown.

"I need to see President Banana urgently," she instructed the yellow-faced guard. She refused to give a reason, stressing it was of the 'utmost urgency'. She liked saying 'utmost' and decided to use it more often in the future because it was an 'Alec sort of a word'.

"Would Advisor Rachel please wait here?" the guard politely replied before disappearing inside the palace. He took ages. After finally re-emerging, he explained: "I'm afraid there'll be a bit of a delay. The First Lady Violet is looking for her violet nail polish. I'll send a messenger to tell you when... um—"

When he saw Rachel's expression change from cross to livid, he stopped and nervously fingered the lapels on his uniform.

"This is extremely urgent!" the girl insisted, worrying that the tea might get cold. "Has she checked inside her purse?"

"I shall relay your advice to First Lady Violet immediately," the guard promised. He hurried back into the palace and quickly returned.

"The President and the First Lady will receive you now, Advisor Rachel."

The guard was far too slow, so Rachel ran on ahead of him, up the wide stairway and into the Great Hall where President Banana and First Lady Violet were seated on large gold, yellow and violet-cushioned chairs. Their cheesy grins suggested they thought they were about to have an important photograph taken of them, seated together, because the Colorwallies had won the war. The President stood and gave the girl a presidential bow. Rachel bowed back. She now felt a rather nervous in the absence of Sheriff Tomato.

"Um," she began, then, "Erm..."

"An excellent idea! Truly amazing. What a brilliant military advisor we have, my dear. Absolutely brilliant. And yes, do tidy up your nails, dearest, for the big picture in the newspaper. Please do."

Although the President was addressing his wife, the violet coloured woman seemed far too absorbed with her freshly painted nails to pay him any attention. Somehow this gave Rachel the courage to continue...

"You're... um... both invited to a tea-party," she said. "To celebrate. It's on the bridge. And you can have some of Mrs Pink's cake when you've signed a special form."

"Oh, I do love cake!" exclaimed President Banana, gleefully rubbing his hands. "We'll come as soon as my good lady has sorted out her nails. But what about the photo?"

Rachel uttered an exasperated sigh.

"Not yet! And please hurry!" she urged. "The tea will get cold. The photo can come later. If anyone's got a camera."

"Oh, we mustn't have cold tea, must we, Violet?"

"In her purse?" Rachel suggested when she saw the First Lady peering around, as if searching for something.

"What?" asked the President.

"First Lady Violet's nail polish. I expect it's in her purse."

"Did you hear that, my dear? In your purse! What a clever military advisor we have!"

"Oh *do* hurry up! On the bridge, remember," Rachel reminded them before turning to take her leave. She ran back along the corridor, down the stairs and out through the grand door where she nearly knocked over the yellow-faced guard.

At the bridge, the tea-party was well under way. Alec, looking *almost* handsome with a clean face, was helping to pour cups of tea, and Lieutenant Whitestone was assisting Mrs Pink by cutting the cake and handing out slices on plates. All the important people, apart from the absent Colorwally presidential couple, were already tucking in. Even General Greengage, having finally been persuaded to leave his brushes in neat little piles on the bridge wall. Mrs Pink winked at Rachel when the girl offered to help with the cake.

"We're getting along very nicely, aren't we, Lieutenant Whitestone?" she said.

The man beside her beamed a kind smile, but Rachel had a sneaky feeling that this was really meant for Mrs

Pink.

"Another thing, Rachel. Look!"

Mrs Pink showed Rachel the Treaty of Waffles. Everyone had signed, except for the girl herself, Waffles and President Banana. Mrs Pink handed her a pen and, feeling thoroughly proud of her and Alec's achievement, Rachel signed her name above that of her new friend. Waffles made a pink paw print.

"They're here!" someone announced. On turning, Rachel saw this was Sheriff Tomato. Sure enough, when she looked in the direction of the palace, a yellow-faced man and a violet-faced woman were approaching the bridge, arm-in-arm. The sheriff ran off to greet them, but President Banana only had eyes for the cake. Ignoring his sheriff, he approached Mrs Pink's table looking rather upset, for there wasn't much left.

"No problem, Mr President," said Mrs Pink. "Just sign here and you and First Lady Violet can have the last two slices."

Without reading what he was signing, President Banana hurriedly added his signature to the treaty in a squiggly script, then began to tuck into a generous slice of cake. Suddenly, he noticed an equal mix of Colorwallies and Dullabillies at the party and frowned. He had assumed the party was to celebrate a Colorwally victory.

"Aw ober den?" he mumbled to President Coalface, who had just finished his slice, through a mouthful of cake. The other president shrugged his shoulders, not understanding a word. Maybe he thought that the Colorwallies had invented a strange new language.

"Did be bin de bor?" asked President Banana, his mouth still full, checking that it was the Colorwallies who had won the war.

"I haven't seen any today," replied President Coalface, clearly hoping his answer might be appropriate. Puzzled, President Banana wandered back towards Mrs Pink wondering whether there might be some more cake because it was so delicious. Meanwhile, Rachel overheard Sheriff Tomato talking with Sheriff Nightsky:

"But how come you lot had a paint tank as well?" asked the red sheriff. "It's a highly confidential secret weapon."

"One of our agents got the plans off one of your inventors, I'm told. At a price, mind you. Apparently the man said that at long last he could afford a holiday."

"Can't think who that might be," replied Sheriff Tomato, blinking frantically.

Rachel smiled to herself, thinking of Inventor Lemon sunning himself on a beach on the Costa Amarilla.

Chapter 15

Rachel felt a tap on the shoulder. It was Mrs Pink, and she was very excited.

"He wants me to come and do his washing and cook for them, Rachel. Lieutenant Whitestone! Fancy that. I didn't even have to ask him."

"You'll like his kids," Rachel informed her. "But their granny can be grumpy in the mornings. Best go in the afternoon when she's asleep."

"Thank you. I'll remember. Also, he wants to visit me in my little cottage. He asked whether I needed any repairs done. *Always* lots of repairs to do, you've just no idea!" Mrs Pink winked at Rachel.

"Nerino and Snowdrop still have the brilliant map you drew, so he'll easily find his way to the pink cottage. Well, what's left of the map after Waffles had a bit of a nibble, but I know Nerino will look after it."

"How is he?"

"Nerino?"

"No, Waffles."

"Oh, he's asleep," replied Rachel. "Been a tiring day for him and he's got to get his strength back for the journey."

"Journey?"

"Back to Houston," clarified the girl. "The carousel in the mall. That's how Alec and I got here."

"Oh, but surely you're not going just yet?"

Mrs Pink looked truly upset at the thought of losing her new lodger so soon.

"We really must. Our parents have no idea where we are. They might even have called out the police."

"Who are the police?" asked Mrs Pink. "Do they polish things?"

Rachel laughed.

"Not usually," she replied. "But they do have to know if someone goes missing."

"But you're *not* missing!" the pink woman insisted. "You're here!"

"Well, I'll be missing back in Houston," argued Rachel. "Waffles too."

"Oh dear!" exclaimed Mrs Pink. "I shall miss you both, you know."

Rachel gave her a fond hug.

"Thank you. I'll miss you too," she said. She was about to say '*and* I'll miss your cakes' but thought this would have been impolite.

"So what do we do with that?" Mrs Pink asked, pointing to the Treaty of Waffles lying on the table beside a collection of crumbs — all that was left of her mouth-watering cake.

Rachel had not thought about what to actually *do* with the treaty. Perhaps these little people would start to argue whether it should be kept in Colorwallytown or

Dullabillieville and go to war all over again. Rachel could not bear for that to happen. She went over to Alec to discuss an idea that came to her.

"Brilliant, Rachel!" agreed Alec on hearing the plan and Rachel felt herself flush with embarrassment. Actually, she now thought Alec was rather good-looking.

So, according to Rachel's 'brilliant' plan, they would leave the Treaty of Waffles with the lady in the carousel kiosk at the mall back in Houston. She could keep it safely on neutral territory for their friends in Colorwallytown and Dullabillieville. Rachel then asked Sheriff Tomato to tell everyone at the party, in his most 'authoritative tone of voice' (Alec's choice of words), to keep quiet for an important announcement. When everyone, except for a mumbling General Greengage, had stopped talking, Rachel stood up on the table beside Mrs Pink and Lieutenant Whitestone. Holding up the treaty for all to see, she began her speech:

"This is the Treaty of Waffles signed by the great Presidents Banana and Coalface!"

She then read out the terms of the treaty.

"Funny, but I don't remember signing a treaty," muttered President Banana.

Rachel continued:

"This valuable document is to be kept in a very special location by the lady who takes the tokens at the carousel in the mall, in Houston, Texas, USA."

"Well, I do remember hearing something about Houston," announced President Banana. "Can't think where I heard it, but I'm sure it was quite recently. So

Houston must be an important place, then."

"Shhh!" someone silenced. "Don't interrupt your military advisor!"

"And now Alec and I must say goodbye to you all," Rachel told the crowd.

"But what about the paint tanks?" everyone shouted together.

Rachel looked at Alec. He was mouthing something. It looked like "rides for the children", so Rachel called out loudly: "Rides for the children!" In response, there was applauding and clapping with shrieks of delight from the little ones present. Rachel lifted Waffles out of her pocket so that he could wave goodbye with a paw, and her eyes moistened after she returned him to his cosy hideout in her dress pocket.

"Come on," urged Alec. He could see how fond Rachel had become of these funny little people, and how happy she was to have prevented their war from escalating into anything more serious. The boy courteously helped her down from the table. Such a gentleman! As the girl raised her hand, hesitantly, to bid farewell to her friends, Alec grabbed her arm and pulled her away from the gathered crowd and the troops of funny looking soldiers.

Rachel knew he was right to do this as she felt something cool trickle down one cheek. A tear! They had to leave and, hurriedly turning, she ran with him towards the purple hill.

Chapter 16

On reaching the top of the hill, Rachel and Alec were horrified to see the carousel in frenzied action, whizzing around so fast that just looking at it made them feel giddy. Gradually, the mechanism slowed enough to reveal two people seated upon animals. It came to a halt, and on their side of the carousel a plump man in a multi-coloured coat, purple hat and boots and a turquoise-painted face, climbed down off the Rainbow Animal. At the same time, a dark, shadowy figure alighted from the zebra in the shadow of the other side of the carousel. The man in the multi-coloured coat had an air of importance and his haughty expression was stern and unfriendly.

"Good morning!" he addressed the children as he stepped off the carousel. He was tall for a Colorwally. "I'm looking for a Sheriff Tomato. Take me to him at once! I'm the new military advisor to President Banana of Colorwallytown."

Rachel was so thankful that Alec was with her, for she realised that there are certain things boys are better at doing than girls. She gave him a nudge. Alec drew himself up to his full height, still several inches shorter than the man with the turquoise face and said that it wasn't their job to take him to Sheriff Tomato for they were also military advisors. Besides, Alec said, the man's presence was now "superfluous as there's no longer a war between the Colorwallies and the Dullabillies since the Treaty of Waffles has been duly signed by responsible parties."

Rachel felt proud of her friend with his vocabulary of big words. She particularly liked his use of the word 'responsible'. She thought it had a good ring to it, so decided to write it down in her 'word pad' when she got home. The man with the turquoise face was rather less appreciative of Alec's little speech and went a very strange colour, as if turning deep red underneath the turquoise paint. And then he exploded. Both children stepped back.

"How dare you insult Chief Military Advisor Turkey Cupcake!" he roared.

"I don't know," said Alec timidly.

"Don't know what, little boy?"

"How I dare," came the answer.

Rachel shot her hand up.

"Please, sir!" she said, "I know. It's because Alec is very brave." Alec's face went a dusky shade of pink. "And here's the treaty to prove that he's telling the truth," added Rachel, waving the Treaty of Waffles in front of the unpleasant man.

"Hand that over at once!" demanded Chief Military Advisor Turkey Cupcake, reaching out with a long turquoise arm.

But he wasn't quick enough. Rachel gave the treaty to Alec and shouted, "Run!"

Alec leapt like a deer onto the carousel and jumped up onto the zebra. At the same time, Rachel dodged the horrid man and scrambled onto the Rainbow Animal. Chief Military Advisor Turkey Cupcake gaped in fury as the carousel began to turn and Rachel and Alec moved forwards and up and down on their animals.

"Bye!" Rachel called out, cheerily. "You won't be needed now, so you can take the next ride back to where you came from. Okay?"

Rachel heard the man yelling abuse at her, as the carousel went faster and faster, until he became just a colourful, screaming blur.

The sky disappeared. They were inside the mall again, and the Rainbow Animal went slower and slower. Rachel was soon able to make out her mommy sitting on the bench near the rest rooms, still reading her magazine. She waved when the woman looked up and was thrilled to see her wave back. The carousel music ceased when the Rainbow Animal stopped moving. Rachel looked across at Alec and saw the boy dismount from the zebra. She climbed down, ran to her mommy and gave her a long, long hug.

"Hey," her mother said, "what's that for? You don't normally hug me when you get down from the carousel!"

"Didn't you miss me?" Rachel felt quite disappointed.

"After three minutes? Not really, Rachel." And her mother laughed.

The girl turned and saw Alec waiting beside the carousel. He was holding a sheet of paper, so she knew it had not all been in her imagination.

"Just a moment, Mommy," she said. "I have to see Alec

about something."

"Sure, honey. I'm quite stuck into this story, anyway," she said, patting her magazine. "It's set during the Vietnam War, but you'll not know anything about wars, will you?"

Rachel ran back to Alec and they grinned at each other, neither quite knowing what to say.

"It was all true, wasn't it?" she finally asked. "Please say it was."

Grinning, Alec nodded and showed her the Treaty of Waffles. Rachel glanced back at her mommy and, reassured the woman was still reading her magazine, took Waffles out and showed him the treaty.

"That's the last time you'll see your treaty, Waffles, but just think. Because of this there'll never be another war between the Colorwallies and the Dullabillies. Never!"

Waffles lifted his nose up and twitched it a few times.

"That means he's feeling really proud of himself," explained Rachel, and Alec laughed. The girl liked the way he laughed. Not like the catty giggles of some of her female classmates at school.

"That woman in the kiosk? Shall I give her the treaty now?" Alec asked.

"Sure. You do it," she agreed. "I feel too sad."

She watched Alec walk up to the kiosk, envious of his boldness. The woman looked intently at the boy as they talked together. For one awful moment Rachel thought she detected anger in her expression, but when she saw her nod and take the Treaty of Waffles from Alec, she breathed a sigh of relief.

"All done," the boy said when he returned. "It'll be safe

in her hands."

"Where are your parents?" asked Rachel.

"Dead," Alec replied.

Rachel's jaw dropped. She felt awful as she stood staring at him in silence, wondering how to undo the harm she'd done with her tactless question. Tears appeared in her eyes.

"Oh, it's okay," reassured Alec, touching her arm. "They've been dead for ages. It was a car crash, you know. I was only three at the time. So my Granny and Grampa take care of me. They're over there having coffee."

Moments earlier, she had been so happy about having ended a war, and now it seemed to Rachel that the world had become a bad place. She felt bad for Alec having no parents, bad about asking him an insensitive question and furious with those kids at school who spread nasty rumours about him. Worst of all, she felt awful for not knowing what to say to the boy.

"It honestly *is* okay, Rachel," insisted Alec. "Grampa says we all have to die one day."

Rachel began to stroke Waffles. Sometimes this helped to stop her from crying.

"You can borrow Waffles whenever you want," she said, fighting off the tears. "If you ever need company, that is."

"Only if his owner comes with him," replied Alec, pretending to look serious. "You know, my grandparents think I'm far too big to ride on this carousel. That's why they're over there keeping a safe distance. But they don't know about its magic." Rachel laughed through her tears.

"You're the only other person who does. When I saw you here so often, I used to tell myself, 'Rachel knows about the carousel, you bet she does!'"

"You poor thing, having to talk to yourself. At least *I* can talk to Waffles."

"My grandparents just can't understand why I keep wanting to come back here," the boy added.

"Neither can my mom!" said Rachel, wiping her eyes.

She looked again at the carousel and wasn't too surprised to see the Rainbow Animal was no longer there. The zebra, too, was gone.

"Will you tell her for me?" she asked. "About the magic? My mom, that is. Say it's true."

"Sure!"

"Another thing, Alec. Why d'you always wear grey?"

"Don't know! Granny's a bit old-fashioned, I guess. Or perhaps she reckons it doesn't show the dirt so much."

"Oh!" Rachel felt sure Alec wasn't really dirty.

Alec followed her to where her mother sat reading her magazine.

"Mommy... this is Alec."

The girl's mother looked up and saw a serious-looking boy dressed in grey, standing politely beside Rachel. She got up to shake hands with Alec.

"Hi there! Are you in Rachel's class at school?"

"Yes," Alec replied. "And I'm very pleased to meet you, Mrs Santos."

"Mommy, Alec comes here every week, too," Rachel explained. "To ride on one of the animals. He comes top in all subjects at school but he's not a nerd. Honest! And he

97

knows there's something special about the carousel so it must be okay for me to keep on coming back each week, don't you think?"

"Why, of course it is, sweetie!"

"Actually, Mrs Santos, the carousel is magical, but only Rachel and I know it," added Alec. "It takes you to where the animals come from, and sometimes to other places as well. Like where they have wars and stuff. Rachel and Waf—" Alec stopped in response to a gentle jab in the ribs from Rachel's elbow. Wafting!" he blurted. "Yeah... Rachel was dead cool... um... wafting around, stopping wars!"

Rachel's mommy laughed.

"Rachel wafting? I like it. You amuse me, Alec. Ask your parents if you can come and play with Rachel next weekend."

"Mommy! Alec's parents are—"

"Thank you, Mrs Santos," interrupted Alec. "I don't need to ask. They'd be delighted. So would I. They're always telling me to socialise more."

Mrs Santos gave her daughter a knowing look.

"Now doesn't that just remind me of someone, Rachel? Well, apologies, Alec, but Rachel and I have a bit of present buying to do. Birthdays are so horribly social, aren't they?"

"Thanks, Alec," Rachel whispered when her mother was out of earshot. "So sorry she put her foot in about..."

"Nope! *I* should apologise. Nearly let the cat out of the bag about Waffles."

Rachel giggled.

"You mean 'the hamster out of the pocket'. By the way, have you noticed anything special about my dress?"

"It's pink."

"Yeah, well anyone who ain't colour blind can tell that! What else?"

"It's... um... it fits you? My pants are always way too short!"

Rachel's frown vanished when she laughed again.

"It's posh, you dumb bunny!" she explained. "Like for a celebration. Not just Waffles' birthday but our new friendship!"

"Oh, sure thing, Rachel," agreed Alec staring at her dress. "Friends forever!" he added. And they high-fived together.

Back at school, on Monday, Rachel and Alec made it abundantly clear that they had become friends. The girl put word around that people who believed in witches were pea-brained and that Alec was definitely the bravest boy in their class.

The two had lots to discuss. Although Rachel often spoke to Waffles about the Colorwallies and their paint war with the Dullabillies, *he* could not talk back to her, so it was much better when she and Alec could find a quiet spot somewhere and discuss about Mrs Pink and Lieutenant Whitestone possibly getting married, wonder whether President Banana might be allowed to have any more of Mrs Pink's cake and why poor Sheriff Tomato always blinked when embarrassed.

Alec suggested it was some kind of a 'phenomenon'. Rachel didn't think this was quite the right word, although she didn't say so to Alec. She did not want to hurt his feelings, so decided to write 'phenomenon' in her 'word pad' so that she could think about it at a later date.

There was one thing, however, about which Rachel and Alec were in full agreement. That wars are stupid and need children with commonsense to stop them.

About the Author:

Website: www.olivereadebooks.org

Oliver Eade awoke early one morning with a ghost story in his head. He got up, wrote it down and went back to sleep. The following day he was horrified to see how badly written it was. A month later another story appeared and he spent more time with it. Then another and another, and he's now written over a hundred, of which many been published in collections both for children and for adult readers.

He is particularly fond of that magical space between reality and fantasy, into and out of which children slip so easily. His first young reader's novel, *Moon Rabbit*, links Scotland with mythological China (Oliver's wife is Chinese) through the friendship of two children. The sequel, *Monkey King's Revenge*, came out in 2011. A dark fantasy for children, set in North America, *Northwards*, was published in 2010.

Moon Rabbit was a winner of a Writers and Artists' Yearbook New Novel Competition and long listed for the Waterstone's Children's Book Prize. *Monkey King's Revenge* was a finalist for the children's section of The People's Book Prize, 2012.

Oliver also writes for adults and teenagers. Before writing a ghost story in the early hours changed his life forever, his daytime job was being a hospital doctor.

Reviews of Oliver's other children's novels:

Moon Rabbit

Moon Rabbit will lead children's imaginations to fantastical realms. It is a magical mix enhanced by gentle and ethereal illustrations.

Mairi Hedderwick, author of the Katie Morag books.

Northwards

After thoroughly enjoying and reviewing Moon Rabbit by Oliver Eade last year, I was excited to read his new book Northwards. I was certainly not disappointed. Northwards tells the thrilling tale of schoolgirl Jenny on her courageous mission to the icy summits of the Arctic where she must battle the evil Lord Kranyak and his menacing army with help from some of the curious inhabitants of the mysterious north. This action packed and gripping novel proves that with courage, teamwork and true friendships, good can overcome evil in triumph.

A witty and heart-warming novel packed with adventure, this is the perfect gift for book lovers aged 9-14.

Jessica Francis, Sunday Express 'The Cool Zone', Jan 2010.

Monkey King's Revenge (sequel to Moon Rabbit)

Oliver Eade weaves exciting mythology into a vibrantly real

contemporary story. The characters are compassionately drawn, as well as being full of punch. There is a depth in the magic and its meaning that is more than pure fantasy. Alma Dowle's shimmering illustrations transport us wonderfully into this exotic realm in a way that exactly mirrors the lively and poetic text.

Jan Nesbitt, artist, children's book illustrator and tutor, London Art College.

Website: www.olivereadebooks.org